how i found the
perfect
dress

Maryrose Wood

BERKLEY JAM, NEW YORK

THE BERKLEY PUBLISHING GROUP
Published by the Penguin Group
Penguin Group (USA) Inc.
375 Hudson Street, New York, New York 10014, USA
Penguin Group (Canada), 90 Eglinton Avenue East, Suite 700, Toronto, Ontario M4P 2Y3, Canada
(a division of Pearson Penguin Canada Inc.)
Penguin Books Ltd., 80 Strand, London WC2R 0RL, England
Penguin Group Ireland, 25 St. Stephen's Green, Dublin 2, Ireland (a division of Penguin Books Ltd.)
Penguin Group (Australia), 250 Camberwell Road, Camberwell, Victoria 3124, Australia
(a division of Pearson Australia Group Pty. Ltd.)
Penguin Books India Pvt. Ltd., 11 Community Centre, Panchsheel Park, New Delhi—110 017, India
Penguin Group (NZ), 67 Apollo Drive, Rosedale, North Shore 0632, New Zealand
(a division of Pearson New Zealand Ltd.)
Penguin Books (South Africa) (Pty.) Ltd., 24 Sturdee Avenue, Rosebank, Johannesburg 2196,
South Africa

Penguin Books Ltd., Registered Offices: 80 Strand, London WC2R 0RL, England

This book is an original publication of The Berkley Publishing Group.

This is a work of fiction. Names, characters, places, and incidents either are the product of the author's imagination or are used fictitiously, and any resemblance to actual persons, living or dead, business establishments, events, or locales is entirely coincidental. The publisher does not have any control over and does not assume any responsibility for author or third-party websites or their content.

PRINTING HISTORY
Berkley JAM trade paperback edition / May 2008

Library of Congress Cataloging-in-Publication Data

Wood, Maryrose.
How I found the perfect dress / Maryrose Wood. —Berkley JAM trade paperback ed.
p. cm
Summary: Sixteen-year-old half-goddess Morgan is wrapped up in normal concerns, such as junior prom and parental problems, when she learns that Colin, her Irish love, is the victim of a fairy curse and she must make a deal with a leprechaun to save him.
ISBN: 978-0-425-21939-3
[1. Proms—Fiction. 2. Leprechauns—Fiction. 3. Gnomes—Fiction. 4. Fairies—Fiction.
5. Space and time—Fiction. 6. Family problems—Fiction. 7. Connecticut—Fiction.] I. Title.

PZ7.W8524How 2008
[Fic]—dc22

2007050627

PRINTED IN THE UNITED STATES OF AMERICA

10 9 8 7 6 5 4 3 2 1

For all my BFFs, but especially Laury and Mana, who have shopped with me the longest.

acknowledgments

As ever, I am supremely grateful to my editor, Jessica Wade, and to my agent, Elizabeth Kaplan, for nurturing this book from start to finish. They are both very fashionable women and can frequently be seen wearing perfect outfits, if not always dresses.

Special thanks to illustrator Sarah Howell and designer Monica Benalcazar for another gorgeous cover. Thank you (two words, no hyphen), to copyeditor Jenny Brown for saving my butt countless times, to Heather Connor in publicity, Nicole Rodriguez in copy, and to all the wonderful staff at The Berkley Publishing Group.

To my loved ones who read and offer helpful comments (or sometimes just puzzled looks), and to my friends and colleagues who provide encouragement in other ways large and small, thank you for your patience and goodwill— especially Beatrix and Harry, Rita Wood, E. Lockhart, Sarah

Mlynowski, Wendy Mass, Andrew Gerle, Joe Gilford, Laury Berger, Mana Allen, Ann Morrison and Dave Shine.

Big hugs and a magical thank-you to the awesome readers of *Why I Let My Hair Grow Out*. Your notes and e-mails are fantastic, and you are all my BFFs.

one

"tinker bell *pajamas!*" My sister tammy was the happiest girl in the world. "Look, Morgan! Look what Santa brung me!"

"That's 'brought,' Tammy. Look what Santa *brought* me." Even on four hours' sleep, my mom could hear bad grammar coming a mile away. It was Christmas morning, six a.m. Mom was catatonic on the sofa in her bathrobe, dark circles under her eyes, mumbling about verbs. I was in a similarly groggy condition, except I was on the floor and couldn't care less about verbs. My dad was in the kitchen, making coffee with the desperation of a bomb-squad guy dismantling a detonator that was already ticking: five—four—three—two—

"Snow *White!*" Tammy shrieked. "A Snow White *back-pack*, look!"

Mom and Dad and I were basically trashed, in a festive, ho-ho-ho kind of way. But Tammy was happy and hyper and the living room was a blizzard of torn wrapping paper and ribbon and presents from the mall, and isn't that what Christmas is all about?

I admit, I wasn't feeling much holiday spirit this year. I'd still been stubbornly awake at one a.m., reading in the living room, when Mom tippy-toed down to the basement and hauled all the hidden presents upstairs, gently sliding each one under the tree without making the slightest crinkly paper sound. When I went to the kitchen to get some juice and made an accidental *clink* with the glass, she shushed me like a maniac.

"Don't wake Tammy!" she mouthed. Trust me, waking Tammy was the last thing I wanted to do. For weeks the kid had been threatening to sleep under the tree on Christmas Eve so she could catch Santa in the act. It took me—*me,* magical big sister Morgan—an hour and a half to persuade her to go to bed in her room, and that's only because I promised I'd wait up in her place and take a photo of jolly old Saint Nick himself, delivering his sack of loot.

I knew this was kind of a sucky lie to tell your sister on Christmas Eve, but it was the only way to shut her up. I figured the Christmas morning present-mania would make her forget all about the dumb Santa picture anyway, and so far I was right.

"Look! It's Belle! It's Belle from *Beauty and the Beast*!" Tammy clawed the wrapping paper off one of the smaller packages. "Maybe it's a movie or a computer game! Oh, a book. Well, Belle likes books, I guess. . . ."

"Books are a wonderful present, honey." Mom clutched her head in agony. "Not so loud, 'kay?" Mom's always been a freak about Christmas, especially the Santa aspect. The old gal has it all figured out: Presents from Mom and Dad come in one kind of wrapping paper, presents from Santa come in another. She switches pens and even her handwriting, so the tags that read "from Santa" are written in this big curly script in red marker. It makes you wonder if the woman has ever considered a life of crime.

"Morgan, *look*!" Tammy twirled around the room, as my dad stumbled out of the kitchen holding two mugs of coffee. Black for him, a splash of milk for me. Mom switched to green tea a while back on the advice of some health magazine, but you could bet she was regretting that now.

"Cinderella's Fashion Board Game! Daddy, will you play it with me? Willyouwillyouwillyou?"

"After breakfast," Dad said, leaning heavily against the wall. "After Daddy takes his"—*yawn*—"nap." Mom executed the sneaky middle-of-the-night present drop, but it was Dad's job to take a man-sized bite out of the Santa cookie. He wouldn't drink the milk, though. He just poured half of it down the sink. Dad's commitment to putting on the annual Santa-is-real show stopped where his lactose intolerance began.

"Oooooh, *tickets*! Disney Princesses on Ice! We're going to see the shoooooooooow!" Tammy started skating around the living room in her socks. "How does Ariel know how to ice skate? She's a mermaid."

Good question, I thought, feeling a fresh wave of cranky wash over me. No doubt there were some presents for me under the tree too, but not the one I wanted: about six feet tall, with heart-stopping cornflower blue eyes and a tendency to use off-color Irish slang when excited. His name was Colin. I'd fallen for him like a ton of shamrocks last summer when I was in Ireland, but he was twenty and I was sixteen and *no fekkin' way* was his attitude about that. Plus he lived on the other side of the ocean, and not even Kris Kringle could swing that kind of Christmas surprise.

i had to give Mom and Dad credit: An exhausting amount of planning and effort, lying and deceit went into Christmas at the Rawlinson family's Connecticut abode, all designed to pull the wool over the eyes of a seven-year-old girl whose grip on reality was pretty woolly to begin with. What my parents didn't seem to understand was that even Tammy was starting to get sick of it.

"Santa's not *really* real, though, is he, Daddy?" she'd asked, about a week before the holiday. The three of us were in Christmas central, a.k.a. the East Norwich Mall, shopping for presents for Mom. "He's more *magic* real, right?"

"Of course he's real." No way was Dad gonna be the Santa-killer; Mom would go ballistic. "Where do you think all the goodies come from?"

"Santa's—workshop?" Tammy answered hesitantly, looking around. The sickening quantities of merchandise heaped everywhere we turned seemed to suggest otherwise, unless Santa had a serious collection of credit cards.

"*Is* he real, Morgan?" Tammy turned to me, desperate for a straight answer. In my sixteen and three-quarters years on the planet, I guess I'd acquired a reputation for being blunt. "Is Santa Claus true or not?"

Dad gave me the evil eye, but I had no intention of being the Santa-killer either. Not if I wanted to survive junior year.

"Lots of things are true that people think are not," I'd answered, not looking her in the eye. I was kind of the wrong person to ask at that point, though, after what happened to me last summer in Ireland. No biggie, just me riding a bike across the Irish countryside, finding out I was a legendary half-goddess, undoing a bunch of magical faery enchantments and oh, yeah, finding the love of my life. Colin. He'd probably forgotten all about me by now.

Maybe it was the snow on the ground or all the Christmas-in-Connecticut décor everywhere, but my summer adventure in Ireland was starting to feel very long ago and far away, as if I'd dreamed the whole thing. Maybe that's why all I'd wanted to do on Christmas Eve was stay up late by the twinkling lights of our Christmas tree, reading and rereading the book Colin had given me the day I left Ireland.

The tree was adorned from top to bottom with angels and cherubs and winged, fantastical beings of every kind. The book was called *The Magical Tales of Ireland*.

Great read, if you believed in faeries. Even better if you'd actually met some.

"You couldn't get her a basketball hoop for the driveway? A paint-by-numbers set? A board game that wasn't about *princesses*?"

"She gave me a *list,* Helen. She gave me her list for Santa and that's what she wanted and that's what I got. That princess stuff is all they have in the stores anyway." Dad was driving, and he pulled away from the red light just extra-fast enough to show he was annoyed. "Next year, *you* do the Christmas shopping."

Always a pleasure to be trapped in the backseat, listening to the marital discussions. They'd been particularly juicy the last couple of weeks, ever since Dad had been downsized from his job. It's not like we were out of money or anything. First Bank of Connecticut doesn't lay a vice president off right before Christmas without giving him a fat goodbye check. But who was used to having Dad around all the time? Not me. Not Tammy. And definitely not Mom.

"That's *not* all they have." I could hear Mom shifting into higher gear along with the Subaru. "They have blocks. They have Legos. They have—I don't know! Decks of cards! This princess thing has become an obsession. It's not healthy." Mom nodded in my direction. "Morgan was never like that."

That my mother should hold me up as the poster child for healthy psychological development was a sign of just how much things had changed in my house since the summer.

"Morgan was obsessed with other things." Before I could say, *Make a right*, Dad flipped on the signal and turned onto Sarah's street. I was surprised he remembered where it was. "What about Lamb Chop?"

True. I loved Lamb Chop as a kid.

"Exactly!" Mom would not be stopped. "Lamb Chop was age-appropriate. It wasn't a show about a giggly princess whose goal in life is to twirl around in a flowy pink dress, waiting for some muscle-bound prince to show up."

No, I thought, *it was a show about a middle-aged woman who kept a sock on her hand for company.* "What's wrong with flowy dresses?" I threw out, just to keep the argument stoked after I

left the car. "A dress is just a dress, you know? It's your attitude that counts."

Mom slammed her lips shut, but I knew what she was
thinking. She was thinking that Tammy wouldn't grow up to
be president now because her plastic princess tiara was slowly
turning her brain into glitter.

Dad pulled up in front of Sarah's house. "We'll pick you
up at six." He sighed. "When do you take your road test
again?"

"I can't take it until May, Dad." We'd been over this a zillion times and I knew the rules by heart. "I have to have my
permit for, like, four months before I'm allowed to take the
road test. And I still have to do my fifty hours of driving in-
struction. And even if I pass the road test, I can't have any
friends in the car with me for the first six months of my li-
cense because I'll still only be seventeen."

"For Pete's sake, why don't they just raise the driving age to
thirty?" Dad grumbled. "Soon you'll have to be eighteen to
cross the street unescorted. . . . Damn bureaucrats keep adding
new rules every day. . . . *Grumble grumble grumble* . . . "

"But think of senior year!" Mom cut Dad off in
midgrumble. "By then you won't have to depend on us for
rides everywhere."

"Does that mean I'm getting my own car?"

Deafening silence from the front seat of the Subaru. I got
out.

"Have fun with Sarah," Mom called after me. "Play with
some power tools or something!"

* * *

power tools? please. My former best-friend-forever Sarah was in charge of the planning committee for the junior prom, and that's what this get-together was all about.

A bit of background, here: The East Norwich senior prom was typically held at one of the local snooty country clubs. It was thrown by the PTA in full überprom style, with stretch limos, formal wear, photographers, the whole nine yards.

The student-thrown junior prom was originally a baby version of the senior prom, but over the years it had evolved into a kind of half-prom, half-prank spoof of the seniors' ritzy event. The eighties fashion prom was tolerated by school officials, even with all the slutty Madonna outfits (the boys were no better; most of them came as Michael Jackson or Prince, take your pick). The bathing-suits-only prom was more controversial, with parents complaining about all the skin and students complaining that the pool was kept off-limits.

Strangely it was last year's ASPCA benefit prom, where every attendee went home with an adopted puppy or kitten, that sent the school administration over the edge:

> Because of the eccentric and even subversive junior proms organized in previous years by student-run prom committees, the administration feels the student body can no longer be trusted with this important responsibility. This year the PTA will engage a professional prom planner to coordinate all details, with appropriate student input welcome as always.

Or so said the memo from the principal, distributed to all juniors the first week of school. "'Eccentric'? 'Subversive'?"

Sarah had gone wild when she'd read it. "Just because we might throw a prom that's actually *interesting*?"

With the prom planner on board to make sure this year's bash was nothing more or less than your typical annual festival of teenage girls in flowy princess dresses and teenage boys in search of a six-pack, the prom committee was reduced to offering opinions about food, music and décor, and selling tickets at school. I didn't care. To me, being on the committee was just a way to get some face time with Sarah. Now that she had a boyfriend, her fascination with couples-oriented social events had skyrocketed.

Last year I'd been the one with the boyfriend. I'd been the one who acted like a jerk. To her credit, Sarah had hated Raphael from the start.

He's arrogant and bossy. He treats you like you're not smart. And he'll make you drop all your friends, wait and see.

I didn't get how right she was until after Raphael dumped me on the last day of sophomore year (after which I hacked off all my hair in a broken-hearted tantrum). It would have been nice to have Sarah's shoulder to cry on about that, but I'd let the friendship slide because of my all-Raphael, all-the-time attitude. Now we were slowly building it back. Going to prom committee meetings was a small price to pay.

Sarah's boyfriend, Dylan, couldn't have been more different from Raph. He was a junior like us, smart and nice and genuinely crazy about Sarah from what I could tell. His only flaw was that he could be very solitary sometimes. We'd all learned that when Dylan went off on his own, you didn't follow him around asking what's wrong. He just needed his space.

Also—and I don't mean to sound mean about this, because it's just the truth—he was kind of short.

Now, personally, I have no problem with short. It's just that short guys tend to go after short girls, which Sarah most definitely was not. Sarah was tall—five feet ten-and-a-half inches in her bare feet, with good posture to boot. So it was just funny that she ended up with Dylan. Some kids made cracks about it, but most people thought they were all the more cool for not caring about the height difference. Sarah was one of the star players on the girls' intramural basketball team and Dylan played drums in a band, so that helped in the coolness department too.

(I don't know how it is at other schools, but at East Norwich, if you're already a little bit cool, like Sarah and Dylan, and then you do something potentially uncool, it just makes you cooler than you were before. You have to have that starter cool first, though. Otherwise, no matter what you do, it's just a downward spiral.)

Anyway, Sarah having a boyfriend made her a bit more forgiving of my atrocious behavior last year. Still, when the fall term started, we were awkward with each other for weeks. I guess she wanted to be one-hundred percent convinced that Raph and I were permanently broken up and that I was, maybe not the same old Morgan but a new, older and wiser version of the person she used to think was worthy of being her best friend.

That's BF, not BFF. I was pretty sure the forever part was history now.

* * *

Snacks were another big draw of the prom committee meetings, and the other members, Clementine and Deirdre, were halfway through a huge bag of Cheez Doodles by the time I arrived. Clementine and Deirdre were the kind of slightly creepy best friends who were always, always together. They'd been that way since middle school. At the moment, they even had matching orange lips.

Let's talk about corsages, I prayed, as I took my seat at the dining room table. Unlike my family's oversized, open-plan house, Sarah's house had a nice cozy dining room with French doors at either end so people could sit and talk in privacy. *Let's pick color schemes. Anything but the big, bad question* . . .

"So, who's taking everybody to prom?" Deirdre squealed, like she didn't start every meeting by asking the same fekkin' thing.

"I think Tommy Vasquez is gonna ask me," Clementine confided. "His friend Jordan told me that Tommy wanted to know if I had a date yet. If he asks me, what should I say? Should I say yes?"

"Tommy *is* cute," Deirdre said. "But don't say yes right away. 'Cause nobody knows yet who Mike Fitch will ask. And if he asked you, you wouldn't want to be taken already, right?"

"Oh my God, Mike Fitch!" Clementine fanned herself and pretended to faint. In terms of popularity, Mike Fitch was definitely the rock star of the junior class, but in a good way. Unlike Raphael's egomaniacal reign of terror over the seniors, Mike actually deserved to be popular. He was funny and kind and gorgeous, with pale blond hair and big brown eyes, plus he was the lead guitarist in Dylan's band. The fact that it was a Kiss tribute band just added an extra touch of ironic sex appeal to the guy. Who would guess a good egg like Mike could do such a killer Gene Simmons impersonation?

"You think Mike Fitch might ask *me*? He'd never ask me. Would he?" Clem started to get revved and shoved a fistful of Cheez Doodles in her mouth to calm herself down.

"Nobody knows," Sarah said mysteriously. "Nobody knows who Mike Fitch likes. Dylan says even Mike's guy friends don't know." One major perk of Sarah having a boyfriend was that it gave us a mole in the enemy camp.

"So who, *ummm,* are you thinking, *ummm,* that *you* might go to prom with, Morgan?" I knew Deirdre was *umming* out of pity. It was common knowledge that I'd been damaged, dateless goods since getting dumped by Raph.

"It sucks that you can't go with Colin," Sarah said with a sigh.

"Oooh, who's Colin?" Clem and Deirdre practically pounced on me. There wasn't anybody at school named Colin.

I didn't answer right away and not just because Sarah was right. It did suck. It sucked that Colin was so far away and that he thought I was too young to really be his girlfriend and that, to tell the humiliating truth, I hadn't heard from him in a while.

No, I didn't answer because it was hard to know where to start and what to leave out. Was this a good time to tell the junior prom planning committee that I was part goddess? How might that news go over? I helped myself to a Cheez Doodle.

Cheez Doodle, Snack of the Goddess. That idea made me crack up. Sarah must've thought I was having a breakdown.

"You know? Colin?" she prompted, trying to make me snap out of it. "That guy you met in Ireland last summer?"

"Oh, yeah," I said. "Right."

Like I could forget who Colin was.

two

Colin had written me e-mails two or three times a week in August and September, then once a week in October, then twice in the whole month of November. It didn't take the Global Positioning System in my dad's Subaru to see in which direction this trans-Atlantic correspondence was heading.

Then he sent one really short note in December:

Mor,

How's tricks? Hope the hair's growing in nicely. Dublin City University is ripping yer man a new orifice, I've never been so knackered in me life. Brain's in a constant fog from all this high-class education, either that or I need some vitamins. Must crack some books and grab a snooze.

be good luv—
Colin

And then, nothing. No Merry Christmas, no Happy New Year, no come-back-Morgan-Ireland-isn't-the-same-without-you.

The old Morgan would have curled up in a ball of hurt and disappointment and made up lame reasons why he'd stopped writing. *Run over by a truck—sorry, "lorry." Too busy with school. Out shopping for Christmas presents, including one for me, Morgan, the one and only female person on his mind, despite all the zillions of girls his own age he was meeting at DCU . . .*

After that pathetic exercise had run its obsessive course, the old Morgan might have exploded in a burst of anger and told herself that *Colin sucks*, and maybe written him some fake and cheerful note about her fictional new boyfriend, just to see if it made him jealous.

But that was before the summer. Before Ireland. Before the old Morgan discovered she was really Morganne, the fearless, flowy-dress-wearing, part-goddess legend who had the power to undo enchantments, talk to horses, swim with mermaids and rescue stolen children from the clutches of mischievous faeries.

Obviously I hadn't told Sarah everything about my summer in Ireland. I'd kept it simple and magic-free: *I met this cute guy in Ireland and we really hit it off, so maybe when I'm older . . .*

Like a pal, Sarah had acted all overexcited about Colin, the way friends with boyfriends act when their friends without boyfriends get some temporary scrap of male attention. I knew faeries and mermaids were real, but Colin's feelings for me were starting to feel like something I'd made up. So what if Sarah was nice enough to play along with my fantasy world? Sooner or later the truth would come out, just like with Tammy and Santa.

I sure could use another shot at being Morganne, I thought, as I slammed the alarm on my clock radio off and faced the much simpler truth that winter break was over and I had to get my butt to school. *The old Morgan comes back much too easily.*

"Morgan, I need my Santa picture. Where is it?"

On her first day back at school after the holiday, Tammy made an unfortunate discovery. Over the break, the entire second grade of Idle Hour Elementary had decided that Santa wasn't real—all except Tammy.

But Mom had nothing to worry about when it came to Tammy's future presidential bid. That kid stood her ground in front of twenty-five cynical brats calling her a dumb baby, and she even promised to bring in proof. Why wouldn't she? In her mind she already had some: the photograph I was supposed to have taken of Santa on Christmas Eve. Seems Tammy hadn't forgotten about it after all.

Bloody hell, as Colin would say.

"I don't have it, Tam," I said helplessly. "I didn't actually see him. I'm sorry."

"But you *said*." Tammy's big eyes started to fill with tears.

"Want more yummy pasta? Mmmmm!" Dad lifted the wriggly noodles onto his own plate. Mom was working like a fiend these days and wasn't home yet, so he'd made dinner. He was ridiculously pleased with himself about it too. I mean, come on—spaghetti from a box and sauce from a jar?

It wasn't like he'd mastered the *Joy of Cooking* or anything. "Maybe Santa can't be photographed," he added helpfully.

"What, like a vampire?" This slipped out of my mouth before I had time to shut myself up. Tammy let her spaghetti slither out of her mouth and stared at me like I was driving a stake through Santa's heart, right there at the dinner table.

"Santa is *not* a vampire!" she yelled. "Why are you so *mean*?" The red sauce dripping down her chin made her look somewhat bloodthirsty herself, but I was done making wisecracks. Too late, though. Tammy fast-forwarded to full meltdown and ran off to her room, bawling.

"Morgan, was that necessary?" Dad slurped more pasta and chuckled. "But the vampire Santa idea is pretty funny."

Okay, maybe vampire Santa *was* funny, but getting hammered at school by your whole class was not even remotely amusing. Sometimes it was like Dad had no memory at all of being a kid.

"It's not a joke." I pushed my chair back and stood up. "She can't face all those kids again without some backup."

"There's nothing we can do," Dad declared.

"The kids at school are not going to drop this, Dad! I'm gonna go talk to her." I started for Tammy's room.

"Morgan, don't tell her about—you know," he called after me, and I turned around. He mouthed the word *Santa*. "Let her enjoy it a while longer."

"Does she look like she's having a good time to you?" I snapped. "You'd rather she got teased than you have an argument with Mom, that's all." As soon as I said it I knew I'd gone too far.

He wiped his lips with his napkin, a little too calmly. Ruh-roh. "Fine," he said. "Go tell her, right now."

This was how Dad won fights—he waited until you were being unreasonable and then switched sides. "Tell her what?" I asked, knowing I was beat.

"Tell her," Dad said, putting his elbows on the table and lowering his voice, "that there is no Santa." He sounded awfully chilly all of a sudden. How chilly? Imagine the ambient temperature of Santa's workshop at the North Pole. "If you think it's so urgent that your sister know the truth, *you* do it."

"But—I mean—won't Mom be mad?"

"Your mother's not here right now, is she?"

Mom's not here because you got downsized from the bank and she had to find a bunch of extra clients with sloppy closets for her to organize, I thought. That this misfortune had somehow led to Tammy crying in her room over vampire Santa seemed both unlikely and unfair, but I'd already learned that life could be random like that: First Bank of Connecticut has a bad year, and now I had to be the Santa-killer.

i tapped on tammy's door before going in. She was in her pink Ariel beanbag chair, watching *The Little Mermaid* for the zillionth time to calm herself down.

"Sorry about what I said about the vampire," I said. "It was a joke."

"Not funny," Tammy barked, staring straight ahead at the TV.

"Listen." I sat down on the foot of her bed. "I think

you're old enough to know the truth about stuff. That's why I came in here. To tell you the truth."

"Really?" She clicked the remote to mute the TV and turned around to face me. "About *everything*?" For a heartbeat I wondered if this conversation would skip right over Santa and go straight to boys and sex, but Tammy seemed far more interested in the Santa thing right now.

"About whatever you ask me," I replied. "So if you don't want to know the truth about something, just don't ask. Deal?"

She thought hard. She chewed her lip. "Deal," she said.

"If you're not sure, start with something small," I suggested.

"Okay." This was a big moment in a little girl's life, and we both knew it. She took a deep breath. "Is the tooth fairy real?"

Whew, an easy one. "Totally real," I said. "I've seen her myself."

"You have?" Tammy was amazed. This was not the answer she'd expected.

"I swear." *Tinker Bell too,* I could have told her, but I didn't want her to be afraid to put her new pajamas in the wash or something.

She narrowed her eyes. "What about the Easter bunny?"

I mulled that one over. "Dunno, but probably not," I said finally.

Tammy seemed disappointed, but also excited by her newfound maturity. To know the real deal about the Easter bunny—she was in the big-girl leagues now for sure.

"And the groundhog?" she asked gravely.

That cracked me up. "Of course groundhogs are real, Tam! You've seen them at the zoo."

"I mean on Groundhog Day!" she said, leaping up and pummeling me with her grubby fists. "You know, that thing they do with the shadow?"

"No, that's bogus." I scooted back on the bed to make room for her. "The weatherman makes it all up."

"I thought so!" Tammy cried in triumph. She climbed up next to me. "Let's go in order so we don't leave any out. What holiday comes next?"

"After Groundhog's Day? Valentine's Day, I guess."

"Cupid!" she exclaimed. "Is Cupid real?"

"That's a tricky one," I said, leaning back on the pillows. "Cupid is, like, mythological. That means he's not totally real, but not totally fake either."

"Huh." She frowned. "That *is* tricky. I think I get it, though. And what comes after Valentine's Day?"

What *did* come after Valentine's Day? A swirl of mist clouded my brain. There was some holiday; what was it? Something to do with green. Something to do with Ireland . . .

"Saint Patrick's Day." It felt like someone else's voice was coming out of my mouth. "Saint Patrick's Day comes next."

"Leprechauns!" Tammy knelt on the bed and put her hands on my shoulders. "What do you think, Morgan? Are leprechauns real?"

Now, the thing is, I *might* have seen a leprechaun, when I was in Ireland. I mean, I think I did, but it was just for a second. And this ancient warrior-dude named Fergus had assured me I hadn't, because he said there was no such thing as leprechauns, and he should know, right? Being somewhat magical and mythological himself?

"Leprechauns," I said to Tammy, "are controversial."

"What does that mean?"

"It means people disagree. Most people would say no, they're not real." I smoothed a wrinkle out of the Insanely Happy Pretty Princesses comforter on Tammy's bed. "Personally, I'm not sure."

Tammy's face scrunched up in a thinking-hard kind of expression. "So," she said, "some things are true, some are bogus, some are missological, and some we just don't know?"

I smiled. "That about sums it up."

"Will you watch Ariel with me?" Tammy reached for the remote. With a click, the Little Mermaid resumed belting out her show tune. "Oh!" Tammy wheeled around so fast she almost knocked me off the bed. "Mermaids! They're real, aren't they, Morgan? Aren't they?" I felt every inch of her being shimmering with hope.

"The tail part isn't," I said firmly. "They have green-skinned legs and webbed toes. But mermaids are completely, one-hundred percent real."

"Mmmm," Tammy said, already entranced by the television screen.

She never did ask me about Santa.

three

We could not calculate driving directions between
Connecticut, USA and Dublin, Ireland.

fekkin' online maps. What good were they? No matter how many times I asked the computer for directions between my house and Dublin City University, this lame answer was all I got back. And since the only place on planet Earth I wanted to go was not even a drivable destination, it seemed kind of pointless for my dad to be taking me to Kappock's Driving Academy. He agreed with the pointless part but for a different reason.

"What a racket," my dad muttered, palming the wheel of the Subaru. "They cancel all the driver's ed classes at your school, and now this guy wants five hundred bucks! Maybe I should teach you myself."

A few weeks had passed since the vampire Santa incident,

and Dad and I were more or less on speaking terms again. But this "maybe I'll teach Morgan to drive" kick was a new development and one that I wasn't too thrilled about, frankly. It was because Dad found out that Kappock's charged five hundred dollars for the mandatory fifty hours of training. In his words, "Five hundred bucks saved is five hundred bucks earned," and since his job search was going nowhere fast, refusing to pay for my driving lessons was going to be the most money he'd earned in a while.

But he actually had a point about the driver's ed classes at school. The way Dad explained it to me, the whole original purpose of driver's ed was to make new drivers safer. Then someone figured out that the way to make new drivers safer is to make them older, since eighteen year olds have far fewer accidents than sixteen and seventeen year olds. So the school canceled the classes in the hopes that sixteen and seventeen year olds would continue to take the bus and nag their parents for rides until senior year, at least.

Follow the logic, if you dare: There's no driver's ed in my high school anymore, because the whole original purpose of driver's ed can best be achieved by not having it. Proof that logic does not always make sense.

Anyway, today I was going to Kappock's to see the required gruesome don't-let-this-happen-to-you movie about accidents caused by drunken drivers, but my actual behind-the-wheel training would have to wait until Dad got either a job or a lot more patience.

"I can wait for *real* lessons, Dad," I answered, sweet as pie. "You'll get a job soon and then the money won't matter."

Dad laughed a single loud snort of a laugh, the kind that

meant *The money won't matter when you're the one earning it, kid.* "There are the rules in a book," he said, pulling up in front of the driving school, "and there are the rules of the road. Books and classes can only teach you so much. Remember that."

"I'll keep it in mind, Pop." Before I dashed out of the car I kissed him on the cheek, which shut him up. My dad's pretty funny sometimes. Mom says we're exactly alike, but personally I don't see it.

Unpretentious would be one way to describe Kappock's Driving Academy. Skanky would be another. Metal folding chairs, gray carpet and stained linoleum on the floor, a pull-down movie screen mended with clear packing tape.

"Looks kinda bullet-riddled, doesn't it?" I could hear the familiar smirk before I turned around to see it with my own eyes. "It's good to see you, Morgan." Raph grinned at me like old times. "Ready to get behind the wheel? *Vroom!*"

If I could have *vroomed* far, far away from him, I would have. I'd been doing a bang-up job of avoiding him at school all year. Now it was the first day of February. Would there be six more weeks of winter or an unexpected thaw? Only the groundhog knew for sure.

"What are you doing here?" I said, not very nicely. "You already know how to drive."

"I racked up some points on the ol' license-a-roonie," Raph said, spinning a metal folding chair backward and straddling it, facing me. "I ran a red light in Danbury and got busted. My dad said I had to take a defensive driving class before the insurance on the car goes up."

Like his dad couldn't afford the car insurance. Raph's family was pretty well off, even for East Norwich.

"Good thing we're not in the same class," he added. He had an out-of-season tan, like he'd been on a beach vacation recently or in a tanning booth. "That'd be gnarly, huh?"

"Yeah," I agreed.

"You look nice," he said. "Sophisticated."

I stopped myself before the old Morgan-on-cruise-control panted a grateful, *thanks*. From most people, a compliment is a compliment. From Raph, it was a judgment passed down from the ultimate position of authority. *You look nice* meant *You usually don't look this good; why don't you try harder?* It meant, *My opinion about how you look is more important than yours*. It meant, *The way you look is not about you. It's about what I think of you*.

And you could never complain about the condescension, because then he'd just say: "Most girls like it when a guy says they look nice! What's wrong with you?" It was a tricky game, and one I'd always lost.

For the record, Raphael had reacted with undisguised horror the first time he saw me with my hair chopped off, back in September. "What happened? Did you have chemo or something?" he'd blurted out. Then he inched away, like he thought I might be contagious or still radioactive.

By now my self-inflicted buzz cut had grown into a soft, short pixie. Mom said I looked "gorgeous, like Mia Farrow." The reference was lost on me, I have to admit.

Raph's compliment hung in the air between us. I glanced around. A few other students had wandered into the room, but there was nobody I recognized except Mr. Kappock himself, visible through the glass wall of his office. "Kar-Krazy Kappock" was an East Norwich celebrity, mostly because there were advertisements with his picture on them plastered all over town.

Raph rocked the metal folding chair back and forth, which made an annoying metallic squeak. "I went out with Terry Lindsey a few times, but she talks too much," he offered, like I would care. "So, are you seeing anybody?"

I looked him right in the eye. I was cool, calm, one-hundred percent goddesslike in my ability to gaze without blinking.

"Not a soul," I said. "Right now, I don't see anyone at all."

He got it, after a minute.

Sarah had a basketball game the next day. I went, of course. It was a big deal to Sarah, and anyway, what else did I have to do with my Saturday night?

I did have a paper due for social studies on the differences between Confucianism, Taoism and Buddhism, but every time I sat down to work on it, I kept writing stupid stuff instead:

Confusionism: When you know something but don't understand what you know.

Duhism: When you should know something, but you don't.

Butism: When someone tries to convince you that they know something you don't know, but you don't believe them.

So basketball it was. Girls' basketball was kind of a big deal locally, since UConn was famed for its women's basketball teams and there was real scholarship money at stake for the top high school players. Saturday night's game would be a good one: East Norwich against Old Southport.

"Go, 'Wiches! Go, 'Wiches!" Our girls jogged onto the court, fists in the air, and the East Norwich battle cry went up. It made me imagine the whole team whipping out their broomsticks and pointy black hats and flying around the gymnasium. Why not? Stranger things had happened. At least, to me they had.

I'd spent twenty minutes waiting in line for a hot dog, so I still needed to find someplace to sit. I looked around the gym for a familiar face. Clementine and Deirdre were there, together of course, sitting one row behind Mike Fitch and his A-list crowd of guys. Tommy Vasquez—the one Deirdre thought might ask her to prom—was with Mike's group, but he didn't seem interested in anything except devouring the extra-large carton of popcorn in his lap.

"Morgan! Hey! Sit over here!"

It was Sarah's boyfriend, Dylan. As usual, he was defying conventional notions of coolness by sitting apart from his friends, all the way down front—the better to cheer for his woman.

"I saved you a seat!" he yelled to me. At least I thought that's what he yelled. The pregame noise in the gymnasium was deafening. But then he patted the balled-up coat on the bleacher next to him and made a "come on down" gesture. I fought my way through the crowd to where he was sitting, and he pushed his coat over to make room for me.

"Awesome," he said. "Sarah told me to make sure you got a good seat, if you came."

I smiled, but my feelings were all over the place: I was pleased to know that I still mattered that much to Sarah, sad to think that she thought I might not come, embarrassed to admit that I almost didn't. "That's nice," I said. "Thanks."

"No prob!" he said, eyes locked on the referee. "Sarah says you're like a rabbit's foot: You always bring her good luck—okey dokey, here we go!"

The ref blew the whistle and the first half began. It was a good game from the start, but more interesting to me than the game itself was watching Dylan watch Sarah play.

"Shhhh!" he hissed when Sarah was trying to get posses-sion of the ball, as if a high school gym packed full of crazed fans could be shushed quiet. "Go Sarah! Get it get it get it get it, she got it, go baby go baby GO!" When Sarah jumped high and slam-dunked the ball into the net, and the home team crowd screamed and chanted, *Go 'Wiches, go 'Wiches!,* Dylan looked like he was about to go airborne with pride.

Either the dude really digs basketball or this is a man in love, I thought. He couldn't take his eyes off her. Sarah was oblivi-ous, her concentration totally on the game.

Forsaking my usual too-cool-to-act-like-a-fool attitude, I followed Dylan's example and cheered my brains out for the 'Wiches. When Sarah scored we bounced up and down and slapped high fives. At halftime, Mike Fitch came down to deliver a couple of extra-large Cokes, unasked.

"Nice lungs on you two." Mike handed us the drinks. "You must be parched. Drink up."

"Mike, you know Morgan, right?" Dylan said it in the most casual way, but the odds of me knowing who Mike Fitch was were much greater than the odds of Mike knowing who I was.

"Not well enough." Mike grinned. "We should hang out sometime. Later, sports fans!"

Another girl might have read something into that exchange, but I knew better. Mike was always nice to everyone. Being charming was part of his charm. Go figure.

The 'Wiches won, largely thanks to Sarah's fierce play. I watched Dylan hug her afterward, as she stood panting in her sweat-soaked uniform, and felt something heavy form inside my chest. You could call it jealousy, I guess, or your standard third-wheel feeling. It's just that I wanted somebody to look at me the way Dylan had been looking at Sarah all night. With that kind of devotion, so strong and so real that it wouldn't matter if we had to wait a year or two to be together, even if there was an ocean of oceans keeping us apart.

In the not-so-distant days when my parents were getting along better, my dad used to call my mom Apple—"because she's the apple of my eye," he'd explained to Tammy, who still found it confusing that Mom's real name was Helen and not Mom. I'd always thought that expression sounded gross—who'd want to put an apple in his eye? But now I understood.

I'm always looking at you, is what it meant. *When I gaze out at the world, you're in the middle of everything I see.*

Sarah, Dylan, the girls on the team and all their respective boyfriends went out to celebrate, but I caught a ride home with Sarah's parents. They were chatty and friendly as always, but as they drove off and I stood in the dark on the frozen lawn in front of my house, I felt invisible.

I was the apple of no one's eye.

When i got inside i sat down at my computer and did something I'd wanted to do for a while, but hadn't had the nerve.

Dear Colin,

Happy Groundhog Day.

Kind of a sucky beginning. Groundhog Day, the totally bogus holiday. Yet maybe it was fitting, since it was a totally bogus e-mail I'd written so far:

Happy Groundhog Day. One of the stupider American customs. It involves weathermen dragging unwilling nocturnal rodents into the sunshine and not one person takes it seriously, but we do it every year.

We do it but we don't mean it. Just like this e-mail. Because what I really want to be saying right now is, *Where are you, why haven't you written, do you ever think of me at all, do you remember what it was like be-*

*tween us over the summer? How we made each other
laugh and told each other all the stuff that we never tell
anyone? Do you remember the way we kissed on the
beach before you found out how old I was? I told my
friends about you and they keep asking if I've heard
from you. . . .*

I deleted all that crap and started over, leaving out my pathetic true feelings this time. But then I didn't know what to say, so I looked up groundhogs on the Internet.

Dear Colin,

Happy Groundhog Day! Did you know that groundhog
is another name for woodchuck? Did you know that
groundhogs' incisor teeth never stop growing? Did you
know that groundhogs hibernate all winter?

Is that what you're doing, Colin? Hibernating? Is that
why you stopped e-mailing me, because you're
asleep? Wake up! *Wake up wake up wake up . . .*

Delete, delete, delete. Then, kind of without thinking, I wrote this.

Colin,

Hey. It's Groundhog Day, which is meaningless, but
Happy Groundhog Day anyway.

I miss you. Not hearing from you makes me sad. Are you okay? Please write me.

Love,
Morgan

I almost deleted the whole thing, but instead I deleted "love" so it was just signed "Morgan." Then I closed my eyes and pressed send before I could change my mind.

So what if he thought I was stupid for saying I missed him, when he'd already forgotten all about me? So what if my note made him roll those cornflower-blue eyes with annoyance at being hassled by the silly American girl he'd met over the summer? At this point, what did I have to lose?

I was too anxious now to sit there staring at the screen, so I went to brush my teeth. Then I put on my pajamas and did my math homework and made some notes for the Confusionism-Duhism-Butism paper. Then it was time for bed, but I couldn't resist and checked e-mail one more time before shutting down the computer for the night, all the while thinking, *Don't look, it's only been an hour, he hasn't even read it yet so stop acting like a big needy baby—*

There was a reply.

Mor,

Sorry I've been such a bollocks correspondent. Hard to describe what's going on with me: I'd rather tell you when I see you, which might be sooner rather than later. Surprise, eh?

The big news, then—they're shipping me to your side of the Atlantic in a few weeks. You'll never guess where I'm going, some joint called Connecticut. Know it, wink wink? DCU has some special dealio, a "robotics intensive" course at UConn. Daft name, that—you con, they con, we all con for UConn! But at least it's not bloody Yale, that'd be too much for a country boy like me to bear.

Arriving on 1 March, for two weeks only (must be home for St. Patrick's Day with Grandpap, he made me swear on a pint of Guinness). Will I see you? Hope so.

Colin

four

A herd of wild magical talking horses could not have kept me away from the bus depot to meet Colin. The good news: I was there. The bad news: so was my dad.

"I thought he was traveling with a group. Can't the school send a van or something?"

"If you didn't want to bring me I could've taken the bus." Colin's shuttle from the airport was scheduled to arrive any minute, and Dad's whining was making me feel even more nervous than I already did. "Enough, already."

"How about, 'Thanks, Dad'?" The waiting room was nearly empty, with a smattering of vagrants fishing change out of the vending machines and college students sprawled like starfish, asleep on their own backpacks. "How about, 'I know you've got nothing to do all day, Dad, so I deeply appreciate this completely unnecessary and time-killing trip to the glamorous bus depot'?"

"Dad! Get a grip, okay?" Now I understood why my mom had insisted on sending Dad out of the house. Two months of unemployment and he was starting to go nuts.

"Who is this guy, anyway?" Dad asked. "Is he your boyfriend? Is that what's going on here, and I'm the last to know?"

"No!" I could feel myself blushing like an idiot. "He's— he's Colin, he's just, you know—oh *fek,* there he is!"

"Morgan, watch your language—"

I wasn't listening. I was looking. I'd recognize Colin's springy walk a mile away, but it was nowhere to be seen at the moment. He trudged down the long ramp into the waiting area with his head down, but when he lifted his eyes he looked straight at me, as if he'd known all along where I'd be standing.

A big, weary smile broke across his face. There were dark circles under his eyes, he needed a shave and his hair was a tangle—he was the most gorgeous thing I'd ever seen. He was Colin, in Connecticut. And in three more seconds he'd be right in front of me—

"Mor," he said, letting his backpack slip to the ground. "Look at you. *Look* at you!" He put his arms around me so completely I thought he might pick me up and spin me around, but he didn't. He just stood there, holding me, and I made a wish that clocks in every time zone would stop and let this moment last forever.

"Colin," I said softly. "Hey. Welcome to, you know. America. Connecticut, whatever."

"It's the New World, so they say," he whispered in my ear. Then he let go of me and stood up straight. The nearby trash can overflowed with garbage, with a greasy pizza box balanced precariously on top. "Could use a bit of a tidy-up," he added. "But it's not *brand* new anymore, of course. Ye have to expect a few dings and scratches."

"It's a bus depot." My dad was making his presence known, in his snide fashion. "The Grand Canyon is considerably nicer."

"Mount Rushmore too, so I hear." Colin grinned and extended a hand to my father. "Mr. Rawlinson. I'm much obliged for the lift and the hospitality. 'Tis my sincere pleasure to meet you."

"No problemo," my dad mumbled, suddenly shy. He wasn't used to my friends being so polite, or so grown-up, or so male, or so good looking, I guess. "Let's get outta here."

Even with all the extra hours she was working, my mom had insisted on cooking an elaborate dinner in Colin's honor. I'd begged her not to try to wow him with her attempts at traditional Irish specialties. "Make him something he might not get at home," I'd said. "You know, *our* native cuisine?"

"In Connecticut, that would be root vegetables and pemmican," Dad had suggested dryly.

"We don't eat pelicans!" Tammy screeched.

"The Native Americans did," my dad lied. "Cooked 'em in a stew and served them in their own capacious beaks. Kidding! Just kidding, Tam!" No matter how many times he made Tammy freak out, Dad never learned his lesson. It took a chocolate cupcake and half a screening of *Beauty and the Beast* to make her forget about the poor pelicans.

After hours leafing through glossy cookbooks featuring Connecticut's *other* native cuisine (meaning Martha Stewart), Mom decided to make a photogenic and highly labor-intensive vegetable lasagna drenched in béchamel sauce. You cooked the noodles, you cooked the vegetables, you cooked the sauce, then you put it together and cooked the whole thing all over again. To my way of thinking that was like making dinner four times, but Mom was pretty stoked about it. Not to mention the accompanying salad of arugula, mandarin orange slices and lightly toasted pine nuts. Colin gobbled it all up like a starving man and didn't ask for ketchup once.

"*Mmm*—fantastic—after six months in the dorms I can't tell ye how good it is to have a home-cooked meal. *Mmm* . . ."

"We're so fortunate to be able to get wonderful produce year-round." Mom gestured with an orange slice. "We'll have to take you to Lucky Lou's. Have you ever heard of that store? Such *incredibly* fresh food! A wide selection of organic vegetables too."

She was making me want to die, basically. "They have vegetables in Ireland, Mom," I said, hiding my face in my hands.

"But not so ye'd notice," Colin added, with a wink at Tammy.

The phone rang. "Let the voice mail pick up, we're having dinner," my mom said elegantly. She had a whole different way of talking when there was a guest at the table; it was kind of hilarious to observe.

"But, Mommy, you always talk on the phone during

dinner," Tammy piped up. The point was moot, though, because my dad had already grabbed the receiver.

"Morgan, it's Sarah," he said, handing me the phone.

"Hey, Sarah." I glanced at my mom's tense expression. "We're in the middle of dinner. Can I call you back?"

"Sure! Just tell me: Is he there?"

"Yes."

"Oh my God! Can I meet him? Do you guys wanna come out tonight? Dylan's band is playing at a house party. You're totally invited."

Introducing Colin to my friends would be an entertaining evening for sure, but if I didn't have a few minutes alone with him soon I thought I would lose my mind. "I think tonight would be a bad idea," I said. "He's kind of jet-lagged."

"A wee nap and I'll be ready for action." Colin yawned hugely, like a cat. "Or—pardon me! Another time might be better, come to think of it."

"This week definitely, okay? I can't wait!" I hoped the hyperexcited buzz of Sarah's voice wasn't audible to Colin. "Clem and Deirdre want to meet him. And Dylan does too, of course! They're playing again Friday; you should definitely come then."

"Morgan." My mother's voice was a warning. "Dinner? Remember?"

"Gotta go. I'll call you tomorrow, okay?"

"Tell him I said hi!" She giggled. "Top o' the, whatever."

"Will do."

"Morgan told all her friends you were coming," Tammy confided to Colin. "Morgan doesn't have a boyfriend, you know!"

"Thanks for the update, young lady." Colin rubbed his eyes and grinned. "But I'd much rather talk about you. Are ye single, or married, or playing the field, or what?"

"*Colin!*" Tammy squealed. She was crazy about him already, I could tell. "I am in the *second grade*!"

"No!" He pretended to be shocked. "A bonnie lass like yerself? Ye must be the princess of the second grade, then!"

Mom's face got tense all over again, but I could swear Dad was holding back a laugh.

"Let me ask ye something, your highness," Colin went on. "Do ye happen to play football—soccer, I mean? I hear it's become quite a popular thing in the States."

Tammy nodded vigorously. "Everybody plays soccer after school. I'm not very good, though."

Colin sat back and patted his stomach in contentment. "Fear not, young lady. By the time I'm done coachin' ye, ye'll be ready for the World Cup."

Mom looked much happier at that.

After dinner, my mom couldn't wait to give all twenty of her BFFs the full report on her béchamel sauce, not to mention the family's newly acquired status symbol: *Imagine! Our own private Irish soccer coach!* Finally, a possession that trumped every conceivable Lexus, Prada bag or Ivy League admission her friends could potentially brag about.

"They call it 'football' over there, of course," she prattled into the phone, as Dad cleared the table. "He's here to do a program at UConn. I doubt he'd have time to coach the whole team. . . . No, he's just here for tonight; tomorrow we're bringing him to the dorm. . . . Well, we could always ask, I suppose. . . .

To get Colin away from this embarrassing display, I gave him a tour of the house and showed him where to find towels and stuff. All attempts at a private moment were ruined because Tammy kept scampering after him like a puppy. When it was time for her to go to bed she wanted Colin to tell her a bedtime story; no one else would do.

"Something with magic in it," she declared, looking tiny inside her too-big Tinker Bell pajamas.

"Colin's not a big fan of make-believe stuff," I warned. I knew Colin was as antimagic as only a person who'd been raised in a country full of fantastical lore could be.

"But it's not make-believe! Did you know faeries are real?" Tammy turned to Colin. "Morgan told me. Did you know she met the real tooth fairy? Did you know—"

"If ye don't mind there, Tammy," Colin interrupted, "we'll skip all that faery claptrap for now." He stifled another yawn. "I've got a cartload of stories to tell ye about me grandpap's farm, though. The farm's long gone; they turned it into a bunch of suburban houses with a supermarket and a cinema and a bowling alley. Now Grandpap's an old codger and lives in a flat in Dublin, watching the telly all day. But he grew up on the farm, and a lively place it was too. Do ye like chickens?"

"I *love* chickens!" Tammy cried, as if someone had read her innermost thoughts. "Buk buk buk buk!"

The two of them spent the next ten minutes perfecting the chicken head-bob move and comparing their clucking noises. Tammy's was good, but Colin's was positively lifelike.

I excused myself in the middle of a tale about Sadie, the

one-eyed champion egg-layer, and did one last check of the guest room. It was neat as a pin, and superhostess Mom had put fresh flowers in a vase on the nightstand. I couldn't resist pulling one long-stemmed lily out of the vase and laying it across the pillow (I dried it off first, of course). Because, who knew? Maybe a good-night kiss would be coming my way momentarily. A touch of romance couldn't hurt.

Colin is in my house, I thought, nudging the flower into the perfect, wouldn't-it-be-grand-to-smooch-Morgan-now position. *Tonight he'll sleep down the hall from me, and in the morning I'll wake up and he'll still be here.* If that wasn't proof of magic in the world, nothing was.

When I went back to Tammy's room, Colin was out cold, sprawled across the foot of Tammy's bed, snoring. Tammy was curled up under the covers and only a tiny bit awake herself.

"Good story," she mumbled. "Made us both sleepy."

It took some pretty vigorous shakes to get Colin to the point where I could lead him down the hall to the guest room. Only half-awake, he didn't resist as I pulled off his battered Nikes.

"Sorry I'm so wiped. Must be the time change. . . ." he mumbled. "Haven't been sleeping well, lately . . . Right now I swear I could sleep for a week, though. . . ."

"Want me to tuck you in?" I joked, but of course it wasn't totally a joke.

"I'll manage," he said, letting his head sink back into the pillow. I had to snatch the flower away so it didn't get crushed.

Before I could even say good night, he was asleep.

* * *

by ten-thirty Sunday morning Tammy was starving and whining for breakfast, but Colin hadn't come down yet. Dad insisted we start without him.

"Ten-thirty and still asleep! It'd be even later in Ireland," my dad commented, as he stirred his coffee. "Half the day's wasted."

"Don't be inhospitable," Mom said, ladling out the fruit salad she'd been chopping all morning, which was carefully garnished with perfect circles of kiwi and sprigs of fresh mint. "He's exhausted from traveling."

"He knows about chickens," Tammy said, her mouth full of waffle.

"Need to brush up on my roosters, though. It's well past sunup!" Colin practically jogged down the stairs. "Good morning, everyone! I can't thank ye enough for lettin' me lie in. That was quite possibly the best night's sleep I've had in me whole entire life." He smiled charmingly at my mother. "I hope I didn't cause ye to miss church."

Ha. My mom's idea of Sunday worship was hitting a sale at Lord and Taylor's.

"Morning," my dad said, sounding embarrassed. "Coffee?"

"Hardly feel like I need any, but sure." Dad poured him a cup, and within seconds my mom produced a warmed plate laden with perfectly arranged fruit, homemade waffles and a festive drizzle of raspberry syrup.

"We were planning on doing some shopping today," she said, as we watched Colin shovel the food down. "Would you like to see the mall? It's quite something!" Mom said "the mall" with a special glow, like, "Would you like to see *the Taj Mahal*? Would you like to see *the dead come back to life*?"

Say no, I prayed. *Anything but the mall.*

"If ye don't mind," Colin said, glancing at me, "I'd be more than happy to just enjoy your beautiful home, and relax here for a bit."

"I'll stay home too," I said quickly.

Mom got it right away, but Dad slammed his coffee mug down and pushed back his chair. "Me too. I've been meaning to organize the garage."

At my house, we spelled clueless D-A-D.

"Daniel," Mom intoned, in the low pitch she only used when she was about to boss him around. "I *really* think you should come shopping with me and Tammy. Let Morgan and Colin have a chance to catch up."

"But the garage is a mess—"

"It's been like that for *eight years,*" said my mom, the professional closet organizer and most passionately anticlutter person on the East Coast. "It can wait."

My mom could be kind of a goddess herself, sometimes.

Colin and Morgan... alone at last...

As the sound of the Subaru whisking my parents and Tammy to the mall faded into the distance, my heart started to pound. What to do first? Throw myself at Colin and plant a juicy wet one right on his lips? Tell him how much I'd missed him and beg him to move to Connecticut? Offer him more coffee and wait for him to make the first move?

Colin seemed unsure too. "Ye didn't tell me ye lived in a mansion," he said, wandering through the "great room," as my mom called it, with its vaulted ceiling and total lack of privacy. "It's a bloody big house yer folks've got here."

I tried to match his casual tone. "It's medium sized by local standards, believe it or not. People love big houses in Connecticut."

"Three bathrooms!" He turned to me. "And that's medium sized, eh?" He was standing in front of the sofa. How easy it would be for us to sink down on it together and start making out like ravenous beasts. *How easy it is,* I thought, *to remember exactly what his lips feel like on mine. . . .* Considering that I was a person who'd once traveled thousands of years back in time to the days of Irish lore, why couldn't I just skip ahead a few years and be old enough for Colin? *Why why why . . .*

"Will ye listen to me," he said, catching my gaze. "We haven't seen each other since the summer—"

My arms were around him, and his were around me. "I missed you so much," I murmured.

"And here I am, talking about the—"

"Colin—"

"—plumbing . . ."

I turned my face up to his, eyes closed, ready for a kiss. And it came, tenderly, on my right cheek, where it lingered until Colin gently pulled away.

"There's some stuff I ought to tell ye, I think," he said.

I did not like the sound of that one bit.

"I don't understand." The adrenaline rush of fear was clouding my brain. "Are you saying you're sick?" We were sitting on the sofa, but we weren't making out. Instead Colin was busy scaring the crap out of me.

Colin looked away from me and shrugged. "It'd be simpler if I were. They can't find anything wrong with me. I've been to the infirmary at school and a private doctor as well." He tried to joke, but it was forced. "They all say the same thing: I'm fit as a fiddle, if a bit on the ugly side."

Ugly, ha. Sparkling blue eyes, reddish-blond hair, a faery-dusting of freckles across his face and that naturally graceful, athletic bod. Colin was a hunk. Like mine, his hair had grown longer since the summer. It was softer now and tousled into silky curls. He was thinner, a little paler—he looked beautiful; that was the only word for how he looked.

"Colin, please," I begged. "If you're not sick, tell me what's wrong."

He exhaled and took my hand. "All right. Ye know me, luv, I'm a fairly energetic chap by nature. But soon after I started university, something changed." He shook his head. "I was tired all the time and kind of foggy-headed. It got so bad I even tried cutting out the Guinness."

I smiled at that.

"Ye'll think I'm daft, Mor," he went on, in a quiet voice. "I feel like I almost never get a proper night's sleep—except for last night, here in this house, that was quite the exception—but I have these mad dreams."

My head started to ache. "What kind of dreams?"

He opened his mouth, then stopped. "It's completely nutters. Never mind."

Now the room was spinning and I had to hold on. I put my hands on his strong arms and felt the muscles moving beneath his skin, like there was a lean, wild creature that lived inside him.

"Colin—tell me about the dreams." I wouldn't let him go. "I promise I won't think you're 'nutters.'"

I could see the need to tell someone gathering behind his eyes, like the clouds of a distant, fast-approaching storm. *I know that feeling,* I wanted to say. *When you know that no one will believe you, but you're desperate to tell the truth anyway.* If I didn't have Tammy to tell all my faery stories to, I'd probably have gone nutters myself by now.

"At first I couldn't remember any of it," he began. "The dreams would fade as soon as I woke up. But now I'm starting to hold on to bits of 'em, not that they make any sense." He looked at me helplessly. "In the dream I'm at a party. There's dancing, lots of dancing. Everyone's dressed to the nines."

"Like—a prom?" Lame, I know, but it was the best image I could come up with.

"Yeah, I suppose. But it goes on and on. Every night, all night. A never-ending prom." His voice sank lower. "Here's the truly daft part. Now and then, I find things in me pockets. Mostly pieces of paper—notes, lists. They're in me own handwriting, but I don't remember writing them."

"Wait." I had to ask, though part of me already knew the answer. "You *dream* that you find things in your pockets?"

Colin swallowed hard. "I told ye, ye'd think I was daft. No, Morgan," he said. "The party with the dancing is a dream—I think it is, anyhow—but the stuff in me pockets is real." He reached into the back pocket of his jeans, took out a slip of paper, and handed it to me. "They're all different, but this one's typical."

It was a receipt, from a company called Wee Folk Custom Tailors & Alterations. In a curling script, in emerald green ink, it read:

> One flowy princess dress,
> fit for a half-goddess.
> Payment due upon pick up.
> Satisfaction guaranteed!

"Now, how this got in me pocket's one thing," said Colin, sounding exasperated. "But what on earth would I need with a flowy princess dress?"

five

pissed off does not begin to describe how i felt about what was obviously a major shout-out from my old pals, the Faery Folk. "Wee Folk Custom Tailors!" I exclaimed. "Those fekkin' faeries—"

But the look on Colin's face shut me up fast. Colin believed in Unix programming and a pint of Guinness after a long day's bike ride. He believed that a guy in college should not date a sixteen-year-old girl, no matter how convinced she might be that he was her soulmate and the world's best kisser. But he did not believe in faeries, or leprechauns, or mermaids, or Tinker Bell, or any of that "faery claptrap," as he called it.

I knew without question that his strange dreams, unexplainable fatigue and those bizarre notes were some kind of faery mischief, but there was no way was I going to try to convince Colin of that. At least not until I figured out what kind of troublemaking the Faery Folk were up to.

"Really, Mor," Colin said gently. "Ye didn't used to say 'fek' so much before ye met me, did ye?"

"I know," I said, embarrassed. "My dad is on me all the time—"

"Ye sound like a proper Irish girl, is all." He grinned. "I'm proud to have had such a beneficial influence."

Colin was only too glad not to obsess anymore about his mysterious problems, and we spent the rest of the afternoon gabbing away like we'd never left Ireland. He was full of questions about American high school life, and I wanted to know all about his first year at DCU. A couple of hours passed without us even realizing it, and much too soon my family was back from their shopping expedition. It was time to take Colin to his dorm at UConn.

Dad drove, and Tammy begged to come along for the ride. I was strapped in the backseat with Tammy, and Colin was up front. The whole way to the campus, my dad grilled Colin about the particulars of this robotics intensive.

"It's a competition, really," Colin explained. "They bring together students from all over the world and divvy us up into teams. Then we've got two weeks to build and program a little robot bugger that'll more or less do what we tell it."

"What's a 'little robot bugger'?" Tammy asked.

Colin twisted around to face us. "There's something ye need to remember about me, Tammy," he said, red cheeked. "If I say an unusual word and ye don't know what it means, chances are it's not fit for ye to repeat. Especially at school. D'ye understand?"

"Did I say a bad word?" Tammy asked, delighted. "I thought robots were toys!"

"Well, yes, they can be, of course," Colin fudged. My dad kept driving and said nothing, which was not necessarily a good sign.

"'Robot' isn't a bad word," I explained. "It means machines that move around and do things."

"Oh," said Tammy. "Like the cows and chickens at Lucky Lou's."

"No, no, lass, now I've got ye all bollixed up—I mean, confused." Colin looked at me in desperation. "Cows and chickens are animals. They're not robots."

"They are at Lucky Lou's," I corrected.

"But I thought it was a grocery? The one with all the magnificent veggies?"

"It is," I said, "but it has these animatronic farm creatures too. You kinda have to see it to believe it."

Colin opened his mouth to ask something else, but Tammy interrupted.

"So which word was the *bad* word?"

"*Bugger!*" my dad roared. That shut us up for the rest of the trip.

the UConn dorm was standard-issue state school architecture—a big, institutional-looking box, built in the days when land was cheap and cinder block was plentiful. A far cry from the ivy-covered, Magic Kingdom castles of Yale, but it was good ol' UConn that brought Colin back to me, and I swore then and there to get myself a school hoodie at the campus store out of sheer gratitude.

Dad couldn't find a place to park and Tammy needed to use the bathroom, so she came inside with us while Dad circled. Colin stood on one line to find out where he was supposed to pick up his room key, and I stood on another line for the ladies' room with Tammy.

Watching Tammy do her twirling pee-pee dance dressed in the latest taffeta-and-tiara ensemble made my brain start churning all over again. *One flowy princess dress, fit for a half-goddess.* That dress was meant for me obviously. The receipt was still in my pocket, but what was I supposed to do with it?

And why were the Faery Folk picking on Colin? His exhaustion, his strange dreams, these inexplicable slips of paper—all that needed to stop, pronto. If my pals in the faery realm were trying to get my attention, they'd succeeded. Now I just had to figure out what they wanted.

"Morrrrrrrgan," Tammy sang out, not unhappily. "I can't wait anymore! I need to peeeeeeeee!"

That got us to the front of the line finally.

After i brought tammy back outside to wait with Dad, I offered to help Colin carry his stuff upstairs, though he hardly needed my help. The dorm room was as spare and tiny as a cell. I looked around the four bare walls and wished I could cast some enchantment of my own: sprinkle some magic faery dust that would keep him safe from harm, or at least make sure he got a decent night's sleep.

But my half-goddess talents didn't seem to extend to making magic on purpose. In Ireland I'd only been called on to undo the pesky enchantments of others, and that had mostly involved paying attention and the occasional display of spunk. Could the Faery Folk could even show up in Connecticut? Land of the mall, the McMansion, and the junior prom? It didn't seem possible.

Then again, my standards for what was possible or not possible had gotten a serious ass kicking in Ireland, so maybe I was due for a few more surprises.

Colin dropped his backpack on the narrow bed. It wasn't much more than a cot, really. "Before ye go," he said, turning to me, "there's something I've been meanin' to do."

"What?" I prayed that my breath was still minty from the gum I'd chewed in the car, but Colin only took my hand.

"Apologize. I owe you an apology, Mor, and now's as good a time as any."

"No," I said quickly. "No, you don't."

"Hush, woman!" He smiled. "When all this mad stuff started happening, with the dreams and the notes—I couldn't make heads or tails of it. So I went a bit silent with people. It seemed easier at the time, but only because I didn't know what else to do." He looked at me with his patented mix of goofball charm and utter sincerity. "Ye must think I've gone off the deep end."

"Not any deeper than usual," I teased.

He grinned, and reached for me. But before he could do what I'd been hoping and praying he would do since the moment he'd arrived, an absolute knockout of a girl—think Lucy Liu, age twenty and with an attitude like she'd just won a lifetime membership to Mensa—rapped once on the open door, marched up to Colin, and stuck out a hand.

"Are you Colin? I'm Alice. According to the team assignment sheet, we're going to be partners." Her eyes skimmed me from top to bottom, but apparently she didn't see anyone worth acknowledging because she just kept talking to Colin. "In the competition, I mean. And I hope you're planning to win! Because I'm *expecting* to."

"That's the spirit," Colin said affably. "How d'ye do? A pleasure to meet you, Alice. This is my friend, Morgan."

"Are they letting *children* in the program now?" Alice didn't bother to disguise her displeasure. "How precocious."

"Nope," I answered, giving her my most deadly stare. "I'm just helping Colin move in. Then straight back to kindergarten."

"Right," she said, already tuning me out. "Anyway, Col, we should have a strategy meeting. Compare skill sets. Figure out what our strengths and weaknesses are." She crossed her arms, the picture of impatience. "Anytime you're ready. I'm here to work."

She called him "Col." How gross was that? I thought.

"Skill sets, righty-o." Colin's voice was full of good cheer and a twinge of mockery too, though you'd have to know him to be able to tell. "I'll be with you in a jiffy, Al."

He winked at me, and together we walked down the hall to the elevator. I wished I could stay, or at least give that horrible girl a pinch to shut her up. But my dad and Tammy were waiting downstairs, and I was a half-goddess with some urgent faery sleuthing to do. I'd lingered too long already.

"Good luck," I said. "Have fun at school." I lowered my voice. "Don't take any crap from 'Al.'"

"I can handle her. Thanks for everything, Mor." The elevator arrived, and Colin gave me a quick peck on the cheek. "See ye at soccer practice."

Soccer practice, very funny. Colin had promised Tammy he'd come over the following Saturday to teach her some real Irish "football" moves, guaranteed to destroy any lingering Tammy-is-a-weenie sentiment left over from January's Santa debacle. Second graders might forgive, but they never, ever forget.

Until then he was completely booked, with classes all day and a heavy workload at night. That meant I'd have to wait six whole days to see him again. How insane it was that Colin was so nearby, yet busy doing things that didn't include me! How amazing that I'd see him in less than a week! My emotional repertoire was getting a major workout.

Still, the feeling that burned hottest inside me was frustration: How the fek was I supposed to find Wee Folk Custom Tailors and Alterations? I even looked in the Yellow Pages, but no such place was listed. I'd have to keep my half-goddess wits about me and stay alert for another clue, but for now, the receipt and the promlike nature of Colin's dreams were all I had to go on.

The situation became most painful at that week's junior prom committee meeting where, naturally, the only thing the girls wanted to talk about was Colin.

"Is he as great as you remember?"

"Was it like you'd never been apart?"

"Did he kiss you hello?"

"Did he kiss you goodbye?"

"Has he been seeing anybody else?" That was from Deirdre, and it stopped me in my tracks.

"I—I don't know," I said. "I didn't ask him." He certainly hadn't mentioned such a thing. It sounded like he'd done nothing for months but struggle with schoolwork and his mysterious affliction.

"There's only one question that really matters," Sarah said with authority. "'Is Colin taking Morgan to prom?'" The three of them stared at me like a trio of owls, round-eyed with curiosity.

"He can't." I threw up my hands. "He's only here for two weeks." Colin would be gone by the sixteenth of March; the junior prom wasn't until the twentieth. Right on my birthday, in fact.

Wails! Moans! Many questions were simultaneously shouted into my face—"Can't he stay longer? Aren't you upset? Is it true that Mike Fitch bought you a soda at the basketball game?"—but the interrogation was interrupted by the arrival of the evil prom planner, Mrs. Shirley Blainsvoort of Promfessionals Inc.

As you might expect, she was kind of a freak: bone thin, platinum-haired and so done up with makeup and hairspray that she looked embalmed. Once a month she showed up at our committee meetings armed with questionnaires to collect our "*appropriate* student input," and never for one millisecond did she stop pretending that we were her valued clients, not the students whose God-given right to throw their own weird prom she'd cheerfully snatched away.

"Today, we'll address one of my *favorite* prom topics," she announced gaily, once she'd taken off her twelve layers of pashmina shawls, demanded hot tea with lemon and perched herself on a chair. She'd made the same comment about everything so far: the location, the dinner choices, the type of flowers in the centerpieces—all were her "favorite prom topics." "Today we'll talk about *music*. They say it's the food of love, you know!"

We stared at her blankly. With a tight smile, she passed out a questionnaire.

"We don't need a questionnaire for this," Sarah said. "We know who we want to play at the prom."

"I have a wonderful DJ," Mrs. Blainsvoort cooed. "He's very experienced. He can play any type of music you like."

"DJs suck," Sarah cooed back. "We need live music. We're having a band."

"The problem with *live* music," said Mrs. Blainsvoort pleasantly, "is that the musicians can only play the songs they *know*. And they have to take breaks and bring in all types of *instruments* and what have you. And sometimes, frankly, they're not very good." She wrinkled her nose. "Haven't you ever been to a wedding where the band was just—lame?"

Could anything be lamer than hearing Mrs. Blainsvoort call something lame? She was trying to bond with us now. She must have been scared. She could feel her promfessional control slipping through those bony fingers. For sheer entertainment value, I'd say this was the best prom-planning committee meeting we'd had so far.

"My boyfriend's band rocks," said Sarah, speaking just as pleasantly as Mrs. Blainsvoort had.

"It does," added Deirdre.

"Everybody loves them," said Clem. "The whole junior class wants them to play."

"Your *boyfriend*!" Mrs. Blainsvoort exclaimed. "Well, that settles it. We simply cannot have nepotism. It wouldn't look right. Besides," she said slyly, "wouldn't you rather have your boyfriend dancing with *you* all night? Not jumping around on stage, singing his heart out to every girl in the room?"

In that moment I knew, and Clem and Deirdre knew, that Mrs. Blainsvoort had just made a huge and possibly fatal mistake. I saw Sarah's face change, and we all understood exactly what it meant.

Over her dead body—or Mrs. Blainsvoort's, more likely—would Dylan's band, Ass Your Kiss Goodbye, *not* be playing at the East Norwich High School junior prom.

When i got home there was a funny card from Colin in the mail—the real, U.S. Postal Service mail, postmarked from UConn and mailed the day before. It was a "Happy First Day of Kindergarten" card, and where he'd found one at the beginning of March I couldn't imagine, but that was Colin for you.

Thanks to the magic of e-mail, I'd never seen Colin's penmanship before. Tracing my fingertip over his rounded, sloppy guy-script underscored the fact that the weird notes he'd been finding were unmistakably written in his own handwriting.

The card read:

Mor,

Help! Pris'ner of geekdom here, seeking refuge. Can't get a spare minute on the computers in the lab to e-mail you, all my new schoolmates are too busy plotting the robot rebellion.

Alice is a pip, but not so bad once you get past her personality. Works me like a dog for sure.

Sorry to say the dreams are worse than ever. The all-powerful dorm-lounge coffee keeps me more or less upright during the day, but my mental alertness leaves something to be desired.

Speaking of coffee, enclosed find the latest "Missive from Beyond." Peculiar, innit? I want to check out those robot cows, though, might come in useful for the competition, so perhaps you'll take me veggie shopping after soccer practice.

See you Saturday—wear cleats.

"Coach" Colin

Missive from beyond? With shaky hands I unfolded the note Colin had tucked inside the envelope. It was written in the same loopy scrawl as Colin's card to me, but in emerald green ink, with a dusting of glitter. It read:

> *Having trouble staying awake?*
> *You need a JOLT of caffeine!*
> *Redeem this coupon for*
> *One FREE lucky latte*
> *at lucky, Lucky Lou's.*

six

the double pliers. the back and forth. the jumping Macarena. Each of the soccer moves Colin tried to teach Tammy had a name, and by the time they'd learned a few different ones, it was like the two of them were speaking their own language.

"That's it, girl, now give me the Fake and Turn! Good, now dribble, dribble and nail it with—a False Hesitation!"

"Like this?" Tammy stopped in her tracks and did a strange little dance involving the soccer ball.

"Yes, excellent! Now, Spin-Chop-Spin, and *run* for the goal! Run! Go! That's it! Let's throw in the Reverse Easter Bunny, just to be merciless. . . ."

"Wait!" Tammy wheezed, breathless. "Stop!"

"Stop?" Colin was panting just as hard and so wobbly I was afraid he might fall over. "But we haven't won the World Cup yet!"

"I need a drink." Tammy collapsed and lay on her back on the damp ground. I was freezing in my new UConn hoodie, but the two of them were red-faced and sweating in their T-shirts. Colin reminded me of a sheepdog who'd just been turned loose on the farm after being locked up in a city apartment for months—a blue-eyed hunk of bounding, panting, muddy bliss, except he looked like he was about to pass out.

"I could use a drink meself," he said, his hands on his knees. "Alice is very big on the veggie shakes. She says that's what ails me. A lack of"—he stopped to catch his breath—"zucchini juice and plankton."

I didn't much like hearing him talk about Alice, to tell the truth, but at the moment I was more concerned about how exhausted he looked. "Maybe that's enough for today," I said, offering him a drink of hot cocoa from my thermos. "You should take it easy."

"I know. It feels good to have fun, is all." He took a swig. "Most days it's like I have a constant hangover with no carousin' to blame fer it. Bloody inconvenient."

"I'm tired, Coach," Tammy yelled from the ground. "Can we stop now?"

"Tired! Does Beckham walk around sayin' he's tired? Was Pelé known for complainin' about needin' a snooze?" Colin stretched and groaned. "I'm totally knackered meself. Ready for a hot shower and yer ma's breakfast deluxe. A nap, if I'm lucky. And then, the veggie shopping," he added, catching my eye.

"Yay!" Tammy yelled. "I love Lucky Lou's!"

"Lucky Lou's has its own juice bar, you know," I said. "If it's plankton and zucchini you want, then plankton and zucchini you shall have."

"Brilliant. With whipped cream." He bent over to scoop up the ball and almost lost his balance. I offered an arm for support, but he pulled himself together.

"Off we go," he said, as we started walking back to my house. I stayed right next to him, just in case.

three hot showers and three plates of buttermilk pancakes with sliced honeydew melon and hazelnut-maple syrup later, Colin, Tammy, my parents and I arrived at Lucky Lou's. As we marched across the parking lot toward the entrance, my dad rubbed his hands together like a greedy landlord from a silent movie. "This year," he announced, "I'm going to get a jump on the yard."

Dad loved to garden, or claimed to, but he was always a month or two behind what the season called for. He was known for raking the fall leaves in April and starting tomatoes from seed in June. It wasn't his fault, really. You couldn't work an eighty-hour week at First Bank of Connecticut and keep the yard in top form by sending it frequent text messages.

But Dad was still out of a job, spring was nearly here, and you could see the agricultural ambitions forming in his poor, deluded mind: fifty-pound watermelons! The prize tomato at the county fair! First place ribbon goes to Vice President Farmer Daniel Rawlinson, résumé in one hand, pitchfork in the other.

The vast Lucky Lou's grocery warehouse loomed in front of us. The equally vast lawn and garden department had a separate entrance, over to the right. Dad was already veering in that direction.

"Look at that!" he said, reading the signs. " 'Preseason sale on all garden items!' "

"No gnomes, Daniel," my mother warned. "We don't have room for any more garden gnomes."

"But—they're on sale." His face went slack as he read the sign, and his voice sounded like he was hypnotized. "I'll meet you guys back at the car. . . ."

Unlike Dad, who would stand there for twenty minutes calculating which brand of tomato sauce was cheaper per ounce and then come home with bulk packages of sale items that none of us liked or used, Mom shopped with her eye on the clock. She blazed through the aisles and ticked things off her list like a game-show contestant in a race to the checkout. With Dad safely occupied in the garden department, Mom grabbed a cart, told me to keep an eye on Tammy and took off at a sprint down the aisles.

Perfect. Now Colin, Tammy and I could busy ourselves by tasting the free samples, enjoying Lucky Lou's infamous animatronic entertainments and, most importantly (to me, at least), figuring out how to redeem this magical latte coupon. I wasn't sure what would happen when I did, but I had a strong suspicion I'd be getting more than a free cup of coffee out of it.

Which is why, I thought to myself, *I'd better do it without Colin or Tammy around.* Luckily this place was full of distractions. To Tammy's delight, there was a person walking up and down the aisles in a chicken suit.

"There's a sorry state of affairs," Colin observed. "Poor chap went to drama school with the best of intentions, and now look at him." Then Colin, being Colin, had to go speak to the bird.

"Not exactly like doing the classics, eh, friend? Are you having a grand time in there, or is it murder?"

"'Murder most fowl,'" the bird intoned, "'as in the best it is.'"

"Foul, fowl, I get it," said Colin, delighted. "You're a clever chick, aren't ye? Not every day ye hear the poultry quoting *Hamlet*. Poultry, ham—get it, boss? Me hat's off to ye, bravo!"

The person in the chicken suit couldn't bow because the chicken suit had no waist, but he swayed back and forth, which seemed kind of like a bow.

"Listen to this!" As if we had a choice. Tammy had found the button on a life-sized robotic cow. The button made the cow emit a deafening moo each time Tammy pressed it. After a few *moo*s she got distracted by something above her head. "See!" she cried, pointing up. "They're going to do the song!"

Suspended about eight feet in the air was the animatronic Lucky Lou's Farmhouse Band. Each of the figures was brightly painted, with articulated limbs and the ability to spin and dance in place. A pig played the banjo, a horse played the drums, there was a rooster that smacked a tambourine and crowed on cue and a rosy-cheeked milkmaid swung her bucket and sang:

> *"Lucky who? Lucky you!*
> *"Shopping here at Lucky Lou's!"*

The figurines lurched and danced, their fake jaws chomping up and down to make it look like they were singing, and the tinny song blasted from speakers that were hidden some-place nearby. Tammy clapped with joy.

"Huh," said Colin. "That's givin' me an idea. Mor, can I borrow yer mobile to call Alice? I left mine in the car." I handed him my phone, and watched with displeasure as he typed in Alice's number from memory.

What made me even more unhappy was having to admit to myself that I was jealous. Me! A half-goddess! Jealous of some obnoxious girl who Colin was assigned to do a project with! It wasn't even like they'd picked each other. If she'd been nice to me maybe I wouldn't be feeling this way—but if she were nice, then I might really have something to worry about. . . .

What I need is some coffee, I thought. "I'll be back," I mouthed, as Colin talked robotics with Alice. "Watch Tammy, okay?" He nodded and kept talking.

". . . I don't think we should underestimate the appeal of doing something anthropomorphic. . . . I agree, functional-ity is the primary criteria, but user satisfaction is a crucial component as well. . . . The judges are only human after all. . . ."

Now that I was holding the latte coupon in my hand, I couldn't find a Lucky Lou's employee anywhere. This struck me as odd, since one of the more annoying things about Lucky Lou's was the army of red-aproned, perpetually happy "Luckies" who followed you everywhere, offering as-sistance. Didn't they know that sometimes you just wanted to stare at the Pepperidge Farm cookies in peace and privacy until you decided which kind to get?

I walked to the end of the dairy section and crossed over to the snack aisle, where the potato chips were stacked sky-high. No Luckies. No customers either, which was also odd, because Saturday afternoon was always a zoo at Lucky Lou's, and the aisle where I'd left Colin and Tammy was pretty crowded. Part of me was tempted to go back, just to make sure they were still there, but I had to be brave. Things were getting strange and, based on my experience with the faery realm, that was probably a good sign.

My footsteps echoed on the linoleum as I walked past the beverages and turned into the canned goods aisle. No customers, no staff—no one except the chicken. It was alone now and unobserved, but still in character, diligently scratching for worms on the linoleum floor.

I walked up to it. "Excuse me," I said. "Do you have a latte bar?"

"Whatte?" the chicken said, its voice muffled by the costume.

"Latte," I repeated. "You know, overpriced coffee. Look." I showed it the coupon. "Where can I redeem this?"

It waved one of its stubby yellow wings and started to walk away.

"Do you want me to follow you?" I asked.

The chicken nodded and kept walking. It led me to a set of wide double doors at the back of the store, the kind that looked like they would lead to the stockroom. There was a sign posted on the doors:

Lucky Lou's "Lucky Lattes"
Walk this way

I'd been in this store a million times, but I knew I'd never seen that sign before.

The doors swung open in front of us, and there was a blast of cold air, like we were walking into the freezer section. I tried to go inside, but I couldn't. Despite the cold breeze flowing out, it felt like there was a wall of glass preventing me from going in.

"Walk this way," the chicken said. As it moved, it bobbed its head in a convincingly chickenlike way, and passed through the doors to the other side.

I bobbed my head too, and took a step.

Buk buk buk buk.

This time, I walked right through.

As soon as I did, the temperature dropped about twenty degrees. There were cartons of eggs stacked to eye level on either side of us, and something sharp and crunchy was underfoot.

"What are we walking on?" I asked the chicken. My breath formed little puffs of smoke in the cold.

"Eggshells," it said. It paused, then added, "It's a chicken joke."

Not a very funny one, in my opinion, but I wasn't going to argue.

The chilly, egg-lined passageway abruptly opened up into someplace warm and sunny. We were standing in the far end of an emerald green meadow, and down a gentle slope in the distance was a sprawling, thatched-roof farmhouse and red-painted barn. I heard the honking chatter of ducks coming from near the house. There were sheep dotting the hillsides and a cow grazing nearby. I resisted the urge to go see if the cow had a button that made it moo.

"Are we in Ireland?" I asked. The chicken didn't answer. Then the farmer himself emerged from the barn, cupped his hands around his mouth and bellowed: "Colin! Colin, me boy! Time for lunch!"

"It's a shame the mortals have chopped all this forest down," the chicken commented. "But if you wiggle back in time a bit to when the farm was still here, it's the perfect place to throw a party."

From the tall woods behind me, a little boy, maybe four or five, came scrambling through the brush. He was covered with leaves and mud. For a moment we made eye contact; his were an unmistakably bright and familiar cornflower blue.

"Time for lunch," I said, smiling. He stared at me, open-mouthed.

"You're pretty, ma'am!" he blurted. "I'm goin' to draw a picture of ye! But I must eat first."

Then he took off at full speed toward the house.

He's always been a charmer, I thought. *With a good appetite too.*

"Come," said the chicken, turning its back to the farmhouse. "The party's this way."

I followed the chicken into the woods.

seven

My feathered guide and I walked down a narrow path through the forest. The chicken was clumsy in that big yellow suit, and a few times I had to help it get untangled from branches that had overgrown the trail. After we were well into the dense woods, and the meadow and farm had been left far behind us, I started to hear music, faint but unmistakable, coming from further down the path.

Now, once a person has *buk-buk-bukked* her way through a faery portal in a grocery store, and then finds herself walking through an enchanted Irish forest with a mysterious guide in a chicken suit, you'd expect that any music she'd hear would be in the magical and tinkly vein, right? Flutes, harps—maybe some ethereal, Björk-like vocals?

Apparently not. What I heard was your basic mediocre dance club mix: eighties rock, classic disco, some mild hip-hop and a dash of Meatloaf. The music grew louder as we walked.

Finally we reached a large clearing. Within it were the Faery Folk, hundreds of them, all dressed like the animatronic barnyard creatures at Lucky Lou's. There were farmer outfits, cow outfits, sheep outfits and many different fruit and vegetable outfits. One tall and willowy girl was dressed like a stalk of corn, with her own yellow hair providing the silk that spilled out at the top.

"This costume is amusing, but it does get rather warm inside," the chicken remarked. "I don't know how the real chickens can stand it." Then it lifted off its head.

The chicken was a guy, about my age, fair-haired, with chiseled features and chocolate-brown puppy-dog eyes. He looked a lot like Mike Fitch, actually, but the way he talked reminded me of someone else . . . someone I'd met in Ireland—but who?

"Morganne," he scolded. "Don't tell me you've forgotten me *again*!"

"Oh, *fek*!" I exclaimed. "Finnbar? Is that you?" All too well I remembered the mischievous, spoiled faery boy who'd brought chaos to a kingdom. Finnbar and his clever, maddening enchantments was single-handedly responsible for my adventures in long-ago Ireland last summer. But last summer Finnbar was just a kid, maybe ten years old. Now—assuming this was really him—he was my age, and a hunk to boot.

"Is it me, she asks!" He sighed. "Am I so very unmemorable? Morganne, you do tend to hurt my feelings."

Maybe he wasn't a boy soprano anymore, but that petulant, teasing voice was pure Finnbar. "Sorry," I said quickly. "Of course I haven't forgotten you. It's just that the last time I saw you, you were a little boy."

"Even little mortal boys don't stay that way for long, you know." He smiled. "Children are not allowed at faery balls, and I desperately wanted to come to this one! So I came as myself, but grown."

I didn't get it.

He *humphed* with impatience. "Think, Morganne! You're practically grown. Don't you remember yourself as a child?"

"Of course I do."

"So," he said, as if he were explaining something that was ridiculously obvious, "when I'm a child, why shouldn't I remember myself grown? Honestly, you make everything so complicated!" Finnbar looked at me disapprovingly. "Someone should have told you it's a costume ball, though. You're not really dressed appropriately."

For a guy in a chicken suit, I thought, *you've got a lot to say about other people's outfits.* I looked down, half-expecting to see myself decked out in a floor-length, flowy goddess-gown, suitable for personal appearances in the faery realm, but I was still in the jeans and Converse high-tops I'd worn to Lucky Lou's. My hands flew up to my hair: It was short, not long and wavy and princesslike, the way it had been the last time someone called me Morganne.

"Wait," I said. "In Ireland, I was either Morgan or Morganne. Right now I seem to be both. What gives?"

"Morgan, Morganne, hair, no hair. You place so much importance on externals! And *spelling*! Never my best subject." He giggled, which made his feathers shake. "That little boy from the farmhouse saw you as you really are, though, never fear." Then he frowned. "But your outfit does need—something. Would you like to wear the chicken head?"

"No, thanks." He seemed disappointed. "Listen, Finnbar." I tried to sound friendly. "I would love to hang out with you and catch up. First, though, I need you to tell me what's been happening to my friend Colin."

"But you *did* want a beverage, didn't you?" said a tall, very thin woman, gliding up to us. She was dressed exactly like the milkmaid in the animatronic band at Lucky Lou's, except with too much makeup and a serious case of scary Botox face. Kind of like Mrs. Blainsvoort. "I thought that's why you came!"

Before I could reply, the woman handed me a tall, steaming Lucky Lou's to-go cup. "Your latte, my dear. Two shots, extra foam. Just the way you like it."

"Oh no," Finnbar muttered. "It's Mum."

"We've never had a ball with a *produce* theme before," the woman remarked, as she led us over to the buffet. The food was laid out on the far side of the clearing, on tables made of enormous tree stumps. "It's so *rustic*! Don't you love it?"

A pair of faeries dressed as cantaloupes attempted to waltz past us, but with their round melon bellies they could barely reach each other's hands. "Granted, some of the outfits are not *perfectly* suitable for dancing. But don't they look delicious? I hope you don't mind the recorded music," she added slyly. "This DJ leaves something to be desired, but our usual musicians were already engaged for the evening."

"I don't care about the music," I said. "But who are you?"

Finnbar started to giggle again, as if I'd just said the

funniest thing in the world. His mother shushed him with a glance.

"Silly Morganne," she said. "I'm—"

"Queen Titania!" A pint of strawberries wearing a dangling tag marked "organic" ran over to us. "May I borrow your delightful guest for a dance?" The strawberries held out a hand to me. "Unless you're prone to rashes? Some people find me an allergen, but it's completely unintentional, I assure you."

"Maybe after I finish my coffee," I said, gesturing with my cup. I had no interest in dancing; I just wanted to get the Faery Folk to lay off Colin. But I knew it was best to be diplomatic with these magical types.

"Yes, come back shortly, dear Berrywinkle," said the queen. "The poor girl hasn't even eaten yet. Finnbar, fix Morganne a plate."

Finnbar moved to obey, but his hands were still trapped inside his costume's floppy chicken wings. "Next time, can we *please* have a sit-down dinner?" he grumbled. "Buffets can be so difficult."

"I can help myself," I said, but when I looked at the food I completely lost my appetite. The trays were filled with tiny people, dressed in tuxedos and ball gowns and all creepily realistic. The more I looked, the more I was afraid I would recognize some of them.

"They're made of marzipan," Finnbar explained. "Since the guests are dressed as food, Mother thought the food ought to be dressed as guests."

"It *was* my idea!" said the queen, proudly.

"That's fascinating," I said, turning away from the buffet

before I got sick. "It's a lovely party. But I came here to find out how to help my friend."

"You must mean Colin," Queen Titania said, picking up one of the marzipan people and nibbling at its feet. "He's quite a good dancer, you know. I do hope we see him later, at the evening ball." The queen pouted. "Last Saturday he didn't show up. We were horribly disappointed. It was the first ball he's missed in months."

"He slept at my house last Saturday." I watched for her reaction.

"Well, that explains it," she said, looking at me with glittering eyes. Our 'limo driver' would have had a hard time finding him if he were under your protection. What a pity. Everyone adores Colin. He was sorely"—she took another nibble—"*sorely* missed."

"So," I said slowly, trying to keep the challenge out of my voice, "you've been bringing Colin to your faery balls every night, while he sleeps?"

The queen smiled. "Of course." She made a sweeping gesture that took in the revels around us. "There are so very many faery princesses, you see. And with so many balls to attend, it can be difficult to find a suitable date! We need all the attractive male guests we can find. Colin is quite a catch," she added. "I really must thank you for bringing him to our attention."

"What do you mean?" I knew it was a bad idea to get snotty with her but I couldn't help it. "I never 'brought him to your attention.'"

She looked at me with pity, as if I should already know. "You left your mark on him, Morganne. And surely any man to strike *your* fancy must be a worthy partner for a princess!"

"My 'mark'?" I said, my heart sinking.

"You anointed him with your affection," Queen Titania said solemnly. "You halo'd him with the glimmer of a half-goddess's desire. To the eye of a faery, he shines like a thousand fireflies in the night. All because of you." The queen gobbled up the rest of the marzipan person and delicately licked her fingertips. "He's impossible to ignore, frankly. But I don't have to tell *you* that."

Fek. Could this be any worse? Colin was under an enchantment, and it was all my fault. "I would like to take my mark off him, then," I said firmly. "What do I have to do to make you leave him alone?"

Finnbar sidled next to me. "Morganne," he cautioned. "Perhaps it's time for a dance." But the queen just laughed.

"Silly girl, what a question! Why should we leave him alone? He really has a very good time here."

"He doesn't even remember it," I said. "And it's making him sick. He's human; he needs to sleep."

"No, he wouldn't remember, of course," she murmured. "But we would miss him dreadfully." She picked up another marzipan person off the silver tray. "How charming! This one looks very much like Colin, don't you think, Finnbar?" Before he could answer, the queen bit off the figure's head. "I'd really much prefer you left things as they are," she said to me, her mouth full.

"But if I caused the enchantment," I pressed, ignoring the headless Colin in her hand, "then I must have the power to undo it. Don't I?"

The queen shrugged and viciously shoved the rest of the marzipan man into her mouth. "Mmm, listen! One of my favorite songs!" She started to dance and sing along with the music. "'It's raining men! Hallelujah!'"

That was enough for me. I was out of patience and more than a little pissed off. Plus, I really hated that song. "Finnbar," I said. "Take me home."

Looking glum, Finnbar put the chicken head back on and slowly waddled back toward the forest. I followed, still carrying my now-cold latte.

Behind us, the Queen laughed and danced. "Your question," she called over her shoulder, "has a very *short* answer."

She boogied to the music and threw her hands in the air. "Amen!" she hollered, to no one in particular. "Hallelulah!"

finnbar led me through the woods again, back to the edge of the field. In the distance I saw the farmhouse, now lit from within, a plume of smoke rising cozily from the chimney.

He removed his chicken head once more. "They're nice old humans, that farmer and his wife," he remarked. "I chat with them sometimes. The wife makes me tea. It's pleasant. So few mortals their age can see me. Usually I only have children to play with." Finnbar looked at me quite seriously. "Sometimes I wonder if it's kept me immature. What do *you* think, Morganne?"

Despite my fury at Queen Titania, the thought of Finnbar sipping cups of tea with Colin's granny made me smile. "Immature people don't usually worry about whether or not they're immature," I said. "So I'd say you're doing fine."

He beamed. "What a brilliant observation! You *must* visit

me again soon, Morganne. It's so refreshing to be spoken to kindly. Mother can be—well, I don't have to tell you." He looked at me curiously. "You don't remember her, do you?"

"Should I?" I asked.

He paused, then shrugged. "It's all so long ago—ah, here we are!" The eggshell-strewn path was in front of me; I could see the fluorescent glow of Lucky Lou's like a beacon at the far end. "Just follow the crunchy path." Finnbar waved good-bye with one of his stubby yellow wings.

"Thanks," I said, meaning it. "It was nice to see you again."

"Make sure you finish your coffee," Finnbar urged. "Mother hates it when food goes to waste."

i made my way back, crunching my way carefully along the eggshells. The double doors swung open slowly at my approach. Once I'd passed through they closed behind me, and when I wheeled around and peered back through the glass, all I saw was the stockroom of Lucky Lou's. The store itself was in normal Saturday afternoon mode: noisy and swarming with shoppers and the ever-helpful, red-aproned Luckies.

I was sick of carrying my coffee around, but Finnbar's warning was not to be ignored. *A little caffeine buzz wouldn't hurt right now,* I thought, as I chugged the latte. It wasn't until I'd drained the last sweet slurp that I realized why Finnbar had told me to finish it.

At the bottom of the empty cup were some words:

Shoo = clew

your helpful dredful speling frend,
Finnbar

p.s. — o why don't I jest tell u
yule need to find a ~~liprakon~~
　　　　　　~~leprechawn~~
　　　　　　leprechaun

eight

Colin and tammy were in line at a cash register with my mom by the time I caught up with them, and Colin was on me like green on a shamrock when he smelled the coffee on my breath.

"The coupon was for real, then?" he asked, amazed. "So how in the bloody hell did it get into me trousers?"

"I—I don't know," I answered, which was technically the truth if you ignored the stuff I left out, like the fact that I'd just seen a ticked-off faery queen literally bite Colin's head off and then been instructed to find a leprechaun by a magical guy in a chicken suit. "You know how stores are. Always doing weird things to get the customers' attention."

"Hmmm. Some kind of marketing scheme, maybe," he mused. My mom was arguing with the cashier about whether or not the paper towels were on sale, and Tammy was rocking the shopping cart back and forth to make the wheels squeak.

"P'raps they're paying the Laundromats to stuff people's pockets with adverts," Colin mused. "But how does that explain the other notes I've found? Why the same stunt in Dublin and Connecticut? Seem a bit random, if you ask me."

"Must be globalization," I said, distracted. Mom was getting into something with the cashier.

"It says 'two for a dollar,'" Mom insisted, in her you-don't-know-who-you're-dealing-with voice.

"Only if you buy four," the bored cashier explained.

"I suppose," Colin agreed, but now he was watching my mom too. Her attempt to pay for the groceries was turning into a scene. Tammy cowered behind the grocery cart, her hands pressed against her ears.

"What you're describing is four for two dollars," Mom declared loudly. "Two for a dollar means two for a dollar. Four for two dollars is four for two dollars."

"Isn't it the same thing?" the cashier asked.

"Not if you have to buy four," my mom cried, smelling victory. "It's not the same thing at all!"

She seemed not remotely embarrassed by the incident, and held her head high as she wheeled the grocery cart to the exit. "We have to be cost conscious," she said, to no one in particular. "Until your father finds a job."

On our way out of lucky lou's, Colin took the plunge and ordered a frothy green veggie juice smoothie from the juice bar, with added kelp and protein powder. After one sip he almost gagged.

"Bejaysus!" he cried. "If this potion is all that can cure me of me ills, I'd rather take to me bed with a rosary and pray for the bitter end to come."

Dad showed up at the car just as we finished loading in the groceries. He had two new purchases, one tucked under each arm.

"Two!" my mom cried out. "*Two* garden gnomes?"

"Two was the least amount I could get," Dad explained. "They were having a two-for-one sale."

"No, Daddy, zero was the least amount you could get," Tammy chirped with confidence. "Zero is less than two. It's even less than one!" She turned to me. "Marcus told me there are numbers that are less than zero, but I didn't believe him."

"Negative numbers," I said, buckling her seat belt for her.

"That's what Marcus called them too," Tammy said proudly. "I told him he was crazy."

"Marcus isn't the one who's crazy," my mom muttered dangerously, but Dad just smirked and went around the back of the car to stow his new friends. Unfortunately the cargo space of the Subaru was already crammed full of grocery bags.

"Mind holding the gnomes, girls?" Dad said, passing them through the window.

that's how we drove home: tammy and i each holding a garden gnome in our laps, and Colin nodding off with his head against the window, his tall frame folded up to fit in the backseat while Mom sat up front.

As I sat there hugging my new plastic friend, I thought about Finnbar's secret message. I knew he was trying to be helpful. But where the fek was I supposed to find a leprechaun in Connecticut?

It was an urgent question, but I couldn't concentrate with my parents slugging it out like a pair of Rock'em Sock'em Robot buggers up front. The argument kept up all the way home, continued while we carried the grocery bags into the kitchen and then escalated alarmingly with the combatants finally retreating upstairs to the master bedroom.

Colin seemed to find the squabbling soothing. He kicked off his ratty sneakers and stretched out on the sofa. "I'm glad we've all put aside our company manners," he said with a yawn. "Makes me feel right at home." Then he fell asleep.

I knew he was supposed to be back at school, but I let him nap. A quick afternoon snooze was not going to provoke Queen Titania by messing up the evening's faery ball plans, and after months of nightly dance duty in the faery realm, I knew how desperately he needed the rest.

Dad's gnome collection had started innocently enough. He'd bought one at a yard sale a few years back, "as a joke," he'd said at the time. But, like so many things that begin as harmless fun and end with somebody losing an eye, the gnomes quickly got out of hand. A golf buddy gave one to Dad as a birthday gift. His former officemates started leaving gnome figurines on his desk. It was eBay that sealed his fate by putting temptation within reach twenty-four seven. The man was hooked.

By now there were thirty—make that thirty-two—gnomes in the garage. They spent the winter there, but as soon as the weather got warm, Dad would wake up some weekend morning and declare it The Day of the Gnomes. Armed with dusting cloths, touch-up paint and a bunch of corny props, he'd prepare the gnomes to assume their seasonal positions throughout the yard.

Mom made no secret of hating the gnomes. She said they were a waste of money and, even worse, "the epitome of clutter." Maybe it was the stress of Dad's ongoing unemployment, but today's two-for-one purchase seemed to be setting off the Great Gnome War my parents had been building up to—the one that left shards of fiberglass and threats of divorce in its wake.

Red-faced, white-lipped, my dad clomped down the stairs.

"They're tacky, Daniel!" Mom cried, in close pursuit. "Can't you see that?"

"Two gnomes are tacky," he countered, heading to the fridge. He took out a soda. "Thirty-two is a whimsical collection that screams kitschy charm."

"No, that's *me* screaming," Mom hurled back. "We do belong to a block association, you know."

"Yes we do," said Dad. "And *they* have a sense of humor."

"Not anymore. All your old-timer buddies got voted off the board, remember? This new group is *very* serious when it comes to property values. We could get fined."

"What does 'kitschy' mean?" Tammy asked. "It's not one of those bad words like Colin says, is it?"

"Mmmmph." Colin groaned sleepily from the couch.

"It means tacky," Mom and I said at the same time.

"What about free speech?" Dad pulled back the tab on his soda can until it spit out a wet hiss. "I indulge in a little creative self-expression on my own private property, and I have to worry about getting fined?"

"Mark my words," Mom warned. "If you put that 'whimsical collection' in front of the house this year, the Lawn Police will be paying us a visit."

After Colin's nap—"I swear, the only restful sleep I've had in months has been in this house!" he declared—he was eager to see what the fuss was about, and asked to sneak a look at the gnome collection before heading back to UConn. Mom was burning off stress on her elliptical in the basement, and Dad was burning off stress by driving around town for an hour pretending to look for a newspaper, so I let Colin into the garage and posted myself as lookout in the kitchen. He was still in there when the phone rang. It was Sarah.

"Is he there?" she asked.

"Kind of," I said. "He's in the garage."

"It's teen night at Club Toxins and Ass Your Kiss Goodbye is playing the opening set. They gave Dylan three passes. One for me, one for you, one for Colin. Can you come?"

"I can," I said, "but Colin's about to head back to school."

"You promised we'd meet him this week!" Sarah wheedled. "I really, *really* want you both to come."

"I'll ask him, but I doubt it. He's in a competition, you know."

"Yer man's not just *in* it—he's going to win it!" Colin crowed, walking into the kitchen. Even a short rest had restored some of his old spark. "Those wee friends of yer da's have given me a prize-winning idea. Who're ye jawin' with?"

"Sarah," I said, covering the phone with my hand. "She wants us to come see her boyfriend's band tonight, but I told her you had to work on your project."

Colin looked disappointed. "I do indeed, more's the pity. A band, eh?" He drummed his fingers on the countertop. "What sorta band?"

"They're a Kiss tribute band," I said reluctantly, knowing how much this would tempt him. "Ass Your Kiss Goodbye."

"Dead on!" he cried, delighted. "With the makeup and the dry ice and the long waggly tongues and everything?" Then he frowned. "That's hard to pass up. Damn. Ah, well."

"So?" Sarah asked. "Is he coming or not?"

"He can't," I said into the phone. "Sorry."

"Well, I'll see *you* later at least. If you get lonely you can hang out with Mike Fitch, I guess."

"Mike Fitch?" I blurted. "Will he be there?"

"Well, duh. He's in the band; of course he'll be there. Don't worry, I'm not trying to fix you up or anything. Though I *am* starting to wonder if this guy Colin really exists." Sarah was joking, but she sounded a tiny bit peeved.

Colin checked his watch. "Bollocks, I'd better run for the bus. Who's Mike Fitch?"

"Nobody. Some guy from school. Sarah thinks I made you up," I babbled, while thinking, *Why does Colin care who Mike is? Is he jealous? Do I want him to be jealous? Is that the level of pathetic I've sunk to?*

Colin snatched the phone out of my hands. "Attention, friend Sarah!" he said. "This is the imaginary Colin speaking. If you can hear the sound of me voice, that means you're imaginary too. Cheers!"

He tossed the phone back to me. "Have fun with yer mates," he said. Then he waggled his tongue like Gene Simmons, and left.

Duh. Of course Mike Fitch will be at the club. Dad had dropped me off at Club Toxins, but I was having a hard time working up the courage to go inside, and Mike Fitch was the reason why.

But he'll be onstage, at least some of the time, I thought. And I would be with Sarah. Except I knew Sarah would be completely focused on her adoring drummer boy, the same way Dylan focused on her during her basketball games. And eventually the guys would come offstage and the four of us would be standing there, and there would be witty and possibly flirty banter, and the more I thought about it the more I worried that the evening would really end up feeling like a date.

This was a problem for two totally contradictory reasons, both of which started with the word Colin:

1. Colin was the guy I was crazy about. I didn't want to be on a date with anyone else.

2. Colin might be the love of my life but he was not exactly my boyfriend—yet—and anyway he was going back to Ireland in another week and I had no idea when I'd see him again, and admitting that made me feel kind of horrible. Was I dumb for not wanting to be on a date with a nice, cute guy my own age who lived in the same country as me? A guy who, it must be said, might actually be prom-

date material, once he washed the Gene Simmons makeup off his face? The junior prom was less than two weeks away.

Then I thought of a third, far more serious reason that the date-with-Mike concept was a problem. Reason three also started with the word Colin:

3. Colin was under a serious and potentially dangerous faery enchantment, all because I liked him.

What was it Queen Titania had said? *You halo'd him with the glimmer of a half-goddess's desire.* . . .

The implications of reason number three hit me like a dodgeball to the chest. Would faery mischief happen *every* time I liked someone? If Mike and I hit it off, would he soon come down with a mysterious case of what everyone would assume was the flu, but only I would know was really a symptom of him getting his groove on with some dance-addicted faery princesses all night, every night?

Not gonna happen, I resolved, as I headed for the entrance to the club. I was not liking anyone, and no one was liking me, until I'd undone the enchantment Colin was under and knew how to magic-proof every boy I came into contact with.

Sarah and I stood in front of the stage, the dance floor vibrating beneath our feet, until the band finally took a break. Even between sets Club Toxins wasn't the quietest place in the world to make small talk, but through a series of funny pantomimes, Mike offered to go get me a soda.

After he walked away Sarah yelled in my ear: "I think Mike Fitch likes you!"

"He shouldn't," I said sharply.

Sarah pulled back. "What's the matter? Did Colin finally ask you to make it official?"

I wish, I almost said. But if Sarah was right about Mike, I needed to squash his interest like a bug. *No sparks allowed,* was my new rule. Even the accidental kind.

"Actually I'm getting a wicked headache. Tell Mike I had to go home," I shouted over the music to Sarah. "Please? I don't want to hurt his feelings."

Even in the half-light of the club I could see the skepticism on Sarah's face. "If you don't want to hurt his feelings," she yelled back, "why don't you tell him yourself?"

Across the sea of dancing bodies, I saw Mike weaving his way back to us. Just looking at his unself-conscious smile, his easy grace as he slid through the crowd holding two tall Cokes high in the air—he was no Colin, but it didn't matter; I could feel the pull of his boy-magnetism reach into my core and tug.

. . . the glimmer of a half-goddesses's desire . . .

"I can't," I said, panicking. "I really can't."

Then I bolted out the door.

nine

i stood outside the club, teeth chattering, and called my dad to come pick me up. After I hung up I saw on my "missed calls" that Colin had tried to reach me a few minutes earlier. He hadn't left a message. I called him back and he picked up instantly.

"Hey," he said matter-of-factly. "I called but then I remembered ye were out with yer pals. Are ye home already?"

"On my way," I said.

"An early night, eh? Didja have fun?"

"Some."

"How was the band?"

"Loud." I scanned the area outside Toxins, in case Sarah or Mike had wandered outside looking for me. They hadn't. Sarah had probably decided I was a jerk all over again, and Mike seemed much too sensible to go chasing after a girl who was drama queen enough to leave in the middle of a gig without saying goodbye.

"Did that fella Mike turn up?" Colin asked. He made it sound like a completely innocent question.

"He had to," I said. "He's in the band."

"Ah, good for him. Bein' in a band, that's a proper chick magnet, that is. So, listen, Mor," Colin said, as if we'd been talking about the weather, "the reason I called ye is—I forgot me project binder at your house! Honestly I don't know where me head is at these days."

Chomp. The memory of Queen Titania biting the head off her marzipan Colin came rushing back.

"I'd come over for it now," he went on, "but by the time I got to your place and back on the bus it'd be half past tomorrow, and I'm totally beat, to tell ye the truth. Unless I could stay over?"

Chomp.

If Colin didn't show up at the faery ball again because he was safe under my roof, the queen would be furious. I didn't want to think about what she might do then.

Chomp. Chomp.

"It's too late for you to come over," I said quickly. "But I'll bring the binder to you tomorrow, first thing."

"Could ya, Mor?" he said with relief. "That'd be grand, if ye don't mind comin' bright and early. We've got tons to do, and if I try to slip away again Alice'll have me head."

Chomp. Chomp. Chomp—

Okay, I get the message, I thought. They could be subtle as a pie in the face, these Faery Folk.

"Where did you leave the binder?" I asked.

"In the garage. I was taking some notes about the gnomes, believe it or don't. They've given me a brilliant notion for our wee robot bugger. . . ." He yawned. "'Scuse me! Maybe I should've given the veggie juice a fairer trial, eh?"

"Don't worry. I'll bring the binder to you tomorrow morning." *You should go to bed,* I almost added. But I knew what would happen once he did.

"Yer a peach, Mor," Colin said. "I swear, if me head wasn't attached to me shoulders . . ."

i waited until everyone was asleep before i headed out to the garage to search for the binder. Entering the dark, musty-smelling space in the middle of the night, cold concrete underfoot—it was like landing on a faraway planet.

In the garage, no one can hear you scream. . . .

Bollocks, as Colin would say. I refused to get spooked just by stepping into my own garage. Even if there were thirty-two pairs of gnome eyes staring at me.

The motion-sensing light fixture clicked on as soon as I took a second step. It was mounted up high, in the far corner near the ceiling, and sent long, angled shadows crisscrossing underfoot. Amazing how two-foot gnomes could cast nine-foot shadows under the right conditions.

"Binder, binder, must find the binder . . ." Yes, I was talking to myself, but not because I was scared. It was because—okay, I was totally freaked out! Why the fek hadn't I waited until morning? Wasn't this exactly like those scenes in bad horror movies, where the stupid teenage girl babysitter wanders alone into the basement, dressed in her underwear and carrying nothing but a flashlight, even though there's a psychotic killer on the loose who's been calling her all night and breathing her name creepily into the phone?

Morrrrrgannnnn . . . Morrrrrrgannnnn . . .

The shadows beneath my feet coiled like a tangle of vines. I took another step, willing myself to believe that my foot couldn't get caught, but the shadows writhed and swirled—the ground was spinning, or maybe I was the one spinning, twirling around and around on a dance floor. . . .

"Morgan?" said a voice. "Morgan! Bloody hell, I'm glad to see you! But trust me, lass, you don't want to be here."

Colin stood before me, in his pajamas and with a major case of bedhead, holding a frothy green umbrella drink in one hand and a ballpoint pen in the other. There were no shadows on the ground, just an ornate pattern of black-and-white tile extending across a vast ballroom floor. Around us, hundreds of faery couples dressed in nightgowns and pajamas laughed and danced. At the moment, the music was a swinging big band arrangement of "Rock-a-bye Baby."

"I get it," I said, taking it all in. "It's a pajama party, right?"

"I'm dead serious, Mor." Colin looked around anxiously. "Once they've got ye, they don't let ye go. If ye can still remember how ye came here, ye'd best leave now."

How sweet, I thought. *Colin's the one who's under an enchantment, and all he can think of is me.*

"Don't worry. I can handle the Faery Folk." I watched the adorable stuffed-animal butlers toddle around with trays of canapés. "I've dealt with them before—it's kind of a long story," I added, before he could ask. "Are you asleep right now?"

He shrugged. "In a manner of speakin,' I am. But I'll wake up in the mornin' feelin' like shite, ye should pardon the expression, and I won't remember all this. Just bits and pieces of a dream." He glanced around the high-ceilinged ballroom, with its mirrored walls and crystal chandeliers. "Sometimes I write notes to meself, see? Hold me drink for a minute, I'll show ye."

I took the glass and sniffed the thick green liquid, then wished I hadn't. "Blech! What is it?"

He made a face. "Veggie juice daquiri. Rancid stuff. They're only tryin' to please me, I know, but it never comes off well. Ah, here it is." He pulled a slip of paper out of his pajama shirt pocket and read:

"'Colin old boy, ye spend every night dancin' with the faeries. That's why yer so knackered. Don't be thick-headed now; just believe it. Yours truly, Colin.'"

Colin looked at the note and sighed. "The notes get all bollixed up by morning, but I keep trying." Then he clicked open his ballpoint pen and added, "'P.S., Morgan's here too, fancy that,'" before tucking the paper back in his pocket.

"Would you like another?" A three-foot-tall teddy bear dressed in a tuxedo and carrying a tray was looking up at me with the cutest button eyes.

"No, thanks. But you can take this." I put the disgusting drink on the bear's tray.

The bear nodded. "Nice outfit, Miss Morganne," it said, and ambled off. I looked down to discover that I was wearing a me-sized version of Tammy's Tinker Bell pajamas. No wonder I felt so comfy.

Colin gave me a curious look. "'Morganne'?"

I shrugged. "It's my goddess name."

"Is that part of the long story?"

"Yes, but if I tell you now, you won't remember it anyway." I looked over my shoulder to make sure Queen Titania wasn't nearby. "You know you're under an enchantment, right?"

He rolled his eyes. "So it would seem. But of course I don't believe in such things."

"That's kind of beside the point. Colin, listen." I was starting to feel tingly, as if my time here at the ball was running out. "The Faery Folk love clues and riddles. Has anyone said anything to you that might be a hint about how to undo the spell?" I thought of Finnbar's tip, *shoo = clew*. "Some casual remark—about shoes, maybe?"

"No, not a word." Colin rubbed his head, making his hair stand up at even crazier angles. "You know what's truly humbling about all of this? Knowing that me granny and grandpap were right! All the flack I've given 'em over the years about believin' in the wee folk! I feel like a right eejit now, I tell ye." He shook his head.

"I promise, Colin, I *will* figure out how to break this enchantment." Even to me, my tone of determination seemed at odds with my outfit. "I have one lead already."

His face brightened. "What is it?"

My confidence faded quickly. "I have to, uh, find a leprechaun," I mumbled.

"Bloody hell!" he exclaimed. "Good luck with that." He glanced across the ballroom. "You'd best get out, Mor, before the princess *du jour* comes back from the faery loo. Tonight's contestant is a possessive type. I don't think she'd be happy to see us chattin' away."

I laid a hand on his arm, but as soon as I touched him the room started to swirl. "Don't worry. I'll see you tomorrow morning at UConn. Oh!" I cried, remembering. "Colin, where did you leave your binder? I looked in the garage but I didn't see it. Colin . . . Colin?"

I startled awake, in a cold, shadowy place. Thirty-two sets of motionless, painted-on gnome eyes were staring at me.

Had I drifted off to sleep?

In the darkest corners of the garage I thought I saw something move, but it was the flicker of the fluorescent bulb overhead. I was back in the real world, and the gnomes were just tacky garden ornaments made of plastic and plaster and paint. Nothing more.

It would have been easy to believe that, except for the fact that Colin's binder was now lying directly at my feet, on the cold cement, in a place where I knew it hadn't been before. I reached down to pick it up, keeping one eye on the gnomes at all times.

Hugging the binder to my chest, I walked backward toward the door that led from the garage into the mudroom. I hesitated in the doorway.

"Uh, thanks," I said to the empty garage.

No answer, duh.

Okay, I thought, as I made my way silently upstairs to my bedroom. *What gives?* Two, count them, two trips to faery world had been made today: first at Lucky Lou's and then in my own garage. Both were places I'd been a zillion times before. Neither trip had required any drastic effort on my part—as in, I didn't have to get thrown off a bike while hurtling down a country lane in Ireland with no helmet on. That fateful bonk to the head last summer was how all this half-goddess stuff got started in the first place.

But now my head was totally unbonked. It even had some hair on it. I was in my own hometown, firmly rooted in my own boring and otherwise normal life—all that was different was that Colin was here.

And Colin was there too, I realized, in Ireland, last summer. Was he the key somehow? I sure felt like I was under an enchantment when I was around him.

I didn't look at the binder until I was safe in bed in my room, in my own faded plaid pajama pants and Simpsons T-shirt, my cold bare feet tucked deep underneath the blankets.

I knew it wasn't right to pry into Colin's business, but part of me was itching to know: If I opened the binder, would I find pages of geeky technology jargon and nothing else? Or would there be flirty doodles from Alice in the margins of the pages?

Or maybe I'd find random notes-to-self from Colin, like the ones he scribbled at the faery ball: "Colin old boy, don't forget: Morgan is the girl for you. Spurn all other advances. Regards, Colin."

It had been a long, action-packed and mysterious day, and I was more than ready for sleep, but my curiosity (okay, jealousy and insecurity, whatever) got the better of me. Looking at somebody's school notebook wasn't the same as reading his diary, was it? I mean, he'd never said *not* to look at it. Right?

I took the binder off the nightstand next to my bed and promised myself I'd only take a peek. I never got past the cover, though.

Embossed in gold, on a field of deepest green, it read:

LABORATORY FOR THE
EXPLORATION OF
PRACTICAL ROBOTICS
UCONN

Laboratory. Exploration. Practical. Robotics. UCONN. LEPRUCONN.

I put the binder back on the nightstand. *Thanks for the encouragement, Finnbar,* I thought, as I clicked off the light. *But one of these days, you are going to have to learn how to spell.*

ten

Sarah e-mailed me early Sunday morning.

Prom is in 12 days.
Date may be optional,
but dresses are required.
Shopping = TODAY.
No excuses. Pick u up at 2.

Luv,
Sarah

p.s.
Mike Fitch felt bad about your poor achey head.
Says it's his fault for not bringing you ear plugs.
So there's still hope if you come to your senses!!

At least Sarah was still speaking to me, which was good. But how could I explain to her that I couldn't go shopping for a prom dress today because I'd be too busy scouring the University of Connecticut campus for leprechaun tracks?

The p.s. about Mike I had no choice but to ignore. Realistically speaking, how much fun could I expect to have at prom? I'd be afraid to even talk to anybody at this point, for fear of starting an epidemic of exhaustion and weird dreams among the cute boys of the junior class. Mono Morgan, they'd call me.

I wrote back to Sarah quickly—*Wish I could come, have to go to UConn today, not sure when I'll get back*—

"Morgan!" Tammy ran into my room and started jumping on the bed. She was wearing a poofy pink princess skirt over her grass-stained soccer uniform. "Get dressed and come outside. I want to practice my new soccer moves!"

"Stop jumping, please; it's making me dizzy." I pressed Send on my e-mail to Sarah and turned around. "What's with the skirt?"

"I like it. It's pretty." She fluffed it to maximum poofiness. "Will you practice with me?"

"I would, Tam, but I have to go someplace this morning. Can't you ask Dad?"

"No." She scowled. "He's busy. He said it's the Day of the Gnomes."

"But it's still March."

"It's warm today." Tammy shrugged. "He said the Day of the Gnomes came early because of a 'girl bull warning.' But I don't believe that. There are no girl bulls. Bulls are boy versions of cows."

I had to think for a minute to decode that one. "Global warming, Tam. That's what he meant."

"Bulls don't glow either." She looked somber and lowered her voice. "I think he's trying to make Mommy mad."

Smart kid, I thought. "Ask Mom to practice with you, then."

"Mommy doesn't play soccer." Tammy pouted. "She doesn't like to get dirty."

"Tell her you'll take off your princess skirt if she plays soccer with you," I suggested. "Trust me, that'll work."

So Tammy went off to push Mom's buttons, and I cleaned out my bag to make room for Colin's binder. On impulse, I grabbed the book Colin had given me last summer and put it in there too, to read on the bus.

The Magical Tales of Ireland. I needed to brush up on my leprechaun facts. I was on the hunt, and the more I knew about my prey, the better.

the robotics lab was housed in a large, modern building on the far side of the campus, across a grassy quad and down a tree-lined path past the library and administrative offices. The door was locked and you needed to swipe a student ID card for entry, which I didn't have, so I called Colin on his cell.

"I'm right downstairs," I said.

"Brilliant. Be down in a sec."

I scanned my surroundings as I waited. Where oh where, in this sprawling collection of buildings, was I going to find a leprechaun? *The Magical Tales of Ireland* offered some information, but most of it you'd know by reading the Lucky Charms cereal box: Leprechauns were pint-sized magical shoemakers who smoked pipes and hoarded pots of gold, which they hid at the ends of rainbows. They wore green coats and buckled shoes and funny-looking hats. Sometimes their presence was revealed by the *tap-tap-tapping* sound of their shoemakers' hammers.

The book also said this:

No magical creature is as shy and solitary as the leprechaun. They live alone; furthermore, all leprechauns are male. How the race renews itself is a topic of fierce conjecture.

Considering the above, and taking into account the extreme rarity (i.e., nonexistence) of leprechaun sightings, even highly reputable experts in the realm of Fey studies consider it probable that leprechauns are mythological, rather than magical, beings.

"We should not be surprised that the Fey have their own storehouse of myths and legends," wrote Dr. Thomasina Wetherby, Professor of Faerieology at the Oxbury School of Improbable Research. "After all, even the Faery Folk need stories to tell their wee ones at bedtime." (See unpublished dissertation, 1897, pp. 167–8.)

Or, in my own CliffsNotes version: Leprechauns are either impossible to find or don't exist at all. Not very encouraging.

"Hey," said Colin, flinging open the door to the lab building and almost knocking me off the steps. "Thanks for comin', Mor. Seems I've done nothing but lay trouble on yer doorstep since I set foot in Connecticut."

I handed him the binder and had to restrain myself from commenting on how cute he'd looked in his pajamas the night before. "How are you feeling today?" I asked.

"Woke up exhausted, with the most disgusting veggie taste in me mouth. I'm startin' to understand why they use sleep deprivation to torture prisoners." Then he reached into his pocket. "I found another note this morning. No free coffee this time."

He took out the same piece of paper I'd watched him write on last night, at the faery pajama party. It now read:

> $$$ TEN PERCENT OFF $$$
> Cozy pajamas, all types!
> Flannel, fleece, and fire-retardant
> (As per safety regulations)
> p.s.—footsie styles available!
> *Courtesy of Sleep-Eeze Sleepwear*
> *"Your friend in dreamland"*

"The handwriting could be a coincidence, I suppose. But this isn't any kind of marketing campaign, is it?" Colin was looking at me with an expression I'd never seen on his face before. Not anger. Suspicion, maybe.

"Doesn't seem to be," I said cautiously.

"What is it, then?"

Should I tell him the truth? He'd never believe it, and it would just mess with his head even more while he was trying to concentrate on school. Not to mention he'd think I was insane.

I handed the note back. "Why do you ask me that?"

"I don't know." His bright blue eyes, bloodshot and dimmed by fatigue, searched my hazel ones and came up empty. He turned away from me, antsy with frustration. "Sorry, Mor. I'm just sick of it, is all."

"Things will be better soon," I said. "I promise."

"Yer a mysterious girl," he said, shaking his head. "It's part of yer charm for sure." His weariness showed in his face, but I have to say the rest of him seemed to be in top form. Colin's nightly dance workout was paying off big time in the buns department.

Stop it, I scolded myself. *How can you "unhalo" him of the glimmer of your desire if you keep checking out his butt?*

"Hey," I said, trying to lighten things up, "can I see this robot you're building? And what do my dad's gnomes have to do with it?"

Colin chewed his lip. "I don't think ye ought to come up, actually. Alice will tolerate no distractions. I have to admit, if we win, it'll largely be her doing."

"She's the brains, you're the brawn?" I joked, fighting back my jealousy.

"No, I've got the looks *and* the talent," he said, forcing a smile. "But she's tough as nails, won't quit and she'd rather eat worms than lose. That's what gets the job done, in the end."

He left me with a wink but no kiss, not even on the cheek, and disappeared back inside the building.

Searching the UConn campus for leprechauns was going to take a while. I tried to be methodical. If leprechauns stayed close to their pots of gold, then where would I find pots of gold? I visited every ATM machine on campus, plus the student credit union and the financial aid office. Nothing.

Tapping sounds? I chased woodpeckers all over the quad, and even barged in on some poor guy trying to build bookcases in his dorm room.

I did so many rainbow checks I gave myself a stiff neck from looking up, but it was a beautiful sunny day, with a cloudless blue sky overhead. No sign of rain, no sign of rainbows. There was one false alarm when I saw a flyer posted for a meeting of the Rainbow Student Coalition. I raced over to the Student Center in time to crash the meeting, but it was a bust. Despite the big multicultural buildup on the flyer, the meeting was only for humans.

After a couple of hours of this I'd pretty much convinced myself that there were no leprechauns on campus. Plus I was hot, tired, hungry and incredibly frustrated. *Some half-goddess I am,* I thought bitterly, collapsing flat on my back on the newly green grass of the quad. *Colin is wasting away with exhaustion, and I just want to go home and watch TV.*

Then I remembered what Colin had said about Alice: *She's tough as nails, won't quit and she'd rather eat worms than lose. . . .*

"Fine!" I shouted it to the rainbowless sky. "If Alice can be that focused on a stupid school project, then I can stay focused on saving Colin."

That's when my phone rang. It was Sarah.

"Where *are* you? We're here to pick you up!"

"Didn't you get my e-mail?" I said, flustered. "Sorry, I'm not home; I'm at UConn."

"Excellent! So am I!" She giggled. "We're in the parking lot by the library. Wave, maybe I can see you!"

"But I said I couldn't go shopping today."

"Yes, and I am so ignoring that! You have to get your dress today, dumdum. What if it needs to be altered or something?"

"Sarah, no," I pleaded. "I'm in no mood."

"Shut up," she said cheerfully. "It'll be in all the papers. 'Teenage girl kidnapped and forced to shop for own prom dress.'"

I was too miserable to argue, and my head was starting to ache from the sun. "Trust me," I said, shielding my eyes, "I can't get into *why* right now, but me shopping for a prom dress is kind of a waste of —"

"What? I can't hear you." There was static, and then a beep on the line.

"Fek. Wait, I'm getting another call."

Annoyed, I clicked to the incoming call, half-hoping it was Colin saying, *Never mind about Alice; come up and see my robot and then we'll snog for a bit*, but also just wanting to go home and wallow in defeat.

It wasn't Colin. It was one of those hyperenthused, prerecorded voices, like the kind that yell at you to "Call *now*! For your *free* Disneyworld vacation!"

"Here's a gentle reminder from Wee Folk Custom Tailors and Alterations!" the voice said. "Don't forget to pick up your dress! The management cannot be responsible for items left over thirty days."

I sat up, took a breath and clicked back to Sarah.

"Sorry about that," I said. "Wrong number. Listen, I changed my mind. I will totally go dress shopping with you."

eleven

Shopping with your bf, as anyone who's ever gone shopping with her BF knows, is not just about buying stuff. Shopping is about catching up on gossip, and making fun of the ugly clothes, and telling each other how great you look as you try on things you'd never buy in a million years.

Shopping with Sarah in our true BFF days had always been a blast, and I was secretly glad that my leprechaun-seeking mission was taking a detour to the mall. I would have enjoyed the whole outing even more, except for the fact that the main topic of Sarah's gossip was me.

"Two words, Morgan: Mike. Fitch." Sarah was working her way methodically through the racks of dresses in the eveningwear department of Strohman's Designer Discounts, where her sister had dropped us off. "Prom. Date."

"That's four words," I said, touching the silky fabric of a

slinky black dress with a plunging halter neckline and a slit skirt. "What about this?"

"No," she said decisively. "Too Slutty McSlutface."

"Too 'welcome to my lap dance,'" I agreed. Somewhat reluctantly I put it back.

"Mike likes you," Sarah announced. "Dylan says Mike thinks you are intriguing and original and mad pretty. Oh my God, look at this one! It's like, 'I was a toddler beauty pageant queen.'"

"Who grew up to be an Elvis impersonator," I said absently. "Mike seems like a nice guy. I hardly know him."

"You sort of went on a date with him."

"I thought you said it wasn't a date."

"It kind of was, though."

"I wouldn't have gone if you'd said it was a date."

"Morgan! I am not the ruler of the universe! I invited you, I invited him. You, him, girl, boy, birds, bees. I can't prevent nature from taking its course." She paused and fell into deep contemplation of another dress.

"But I left, remember? I walked out on him. No!" I shrieked, when I saw what she was looking at. "Navy blue? With *white piping*? At prom? No, no, no, no."

"But it's my favorite color."

"Two words for *you*, Sarah," I said. "Shore leave."

Sarah hid the offending dress at the back of the rack where I couldn't mock it any further. "Anyway, why would Mike Fitch even want to talk to me after I ditched everybody at Toxins?" I asked, holding up a strapless magenta number with a ruffled skirt.

"I hope that comes with castanets," Sarah commented. I put the dress back. "Because," she went on, "you are the only girl in North, South, West or East Norwich who doesn't faint in his presence." Sarah turned away from the dresses and put her hands on her hips. "This is all about Colin, Colin, Colin, I know! But Colin won't be here for prom. He's going back to Ireland soon, right?"

"Next week."

"And you're too stuck on him to even *consider* going to prom with Mike?"

"Yes."

"Even though this mythical Colin person is too old for you anyway?"

"He's not mythical," I insisted. "And he's only twenty. It's more like I'm too young for him. I'll be seventeen in less than two weeks," I added lamely, sounding closer to Tammy's age.

"By your birthday, Colin will be, like, a zillion miles away," she declared. "And Mike Fitch is *here*. And he really, *really* wants to take you, Morgan Runaway Rawlinson, to your one and only junior prom, on your one and only seventeenth birthday, the end."

"I don't even know if I can go," I wailed, wishing so much I could tell Sarah the truth. "The whole prom thing is pretty complicated for me right now."

Sarah sighed. "A shmo like Raphael and you fall."

"That was last year," I said quickly.

"A guy who lives in another country, and you're hooked," she went on.

"You haven't even met Colin," I protested.

"I know I haven't, and what is *up* with that?" she said, as if

I were only proving her point. "But a great guy like Mike, who's here and available and interested, and you're a mass of excuses. Morgan, has it ever occurred to you that you are seriously messed up about boys?"

"Yes," I said. "It has."

"I'm just saying." Sarah turned her attention back to the clothes. From the look of concentration on her face I knew she was done arguing and was now focused on finding herself the perfect dress. She was going to prom, even if her idiot friend Morgan decided to stay home and sob into a pint of Ben & Jerry's all night.

We shopped in silence for a few minutes, until I couldn't stand it anymore. I pulled a particularly hideous dress off the rack. "Fine." I tried to sound dead serious. "I will consider going to the junior prom with Mike, but on one condition."

"What?"

"If I can wear this. What do you think?"

She looked the dress up and down, and thought for a full minute. "It's like, Felicity's holiday gown from the American Girl collection got into a slap fight with the BeDazzler from hell," she said, "and the BeDazzler won."

"I was thinking the exact same thing," I deadpanned.

Sarah cracked up so hard that tears ran down her face. If I hadn't been so worried about Colin, I would've joined her.

horsing around with Sarah in the dress store felt so much like old times, I had to remind myself to stay on the lookout for anything having to do with leprechauns or magical tailoring shops. I hadn't noticed anything unusual yet, but since picking up my dress was what the Wee Folk Custom Tailors & Alterations message had instructed me to do, I figured I might as well try some on.

With the help of a shell-shocked Strohman's saleswoman who was clearly already suffering from prom season burnout, Sarah and I gathered up armloads of dresses and camped out in two adjoining booths in the dressing room. Then we took turns changing and stepping out to hear each other's uncensored opinions.

Sarah, who is tall with a lean, athletic build, looked good in almost everything.

I, on the other hand, am medium height with a more curvy shape, and I had a harder time finding something that suited me exactly, but when I did—

"Oh my God!" Sarah practically yelled, when I came out to show her. "Perfect. *Perfect.* That's it. You're going to prom, no arguments. You *need* to be *seen* in *that*."

On tiptoe to simulate the effect of high heels, I walked over to the angled cove of mirrors that had the magical ability to let you check out your own butt. The dress was a pale beige color, just a shade darker than my skin, with a bronze sheen that made it shimmer as I moved. The fabric was substantial but fluid, and hugged every curve closely enough to look amazing, but not so closely as to turn my silhouette into a nightmare of weird bulges and visible panty lines.

I looked in the mirrors, and I had to admit: The three of me looking back had never, ever looked so good.

Behind those three were a zillion more Morgans, all turning and looking and preening in unison. They were reflections of reflections of reflections, and I knew every single one of them was thinking how perfect it would be to show up at the junior prom wearing this dress . . . *and Colin would be in a tux, and together we would slow dance. . . .*

"Nice dress," said the saleswoman. "But not as nice as the one we're holding for you."

I wheeled around. It wasn't the same saleswoman. This one was young and pretty with long black hair and Asian features, just like Alice, in fact, and she was wearing thick-rimmed glasses and an emerald-green apron embroidered with the words, "Wee Folk Custom Tailors & Alterations." Pinned on the apron was a large button that read: "'Wee' make it so it fits!"

"The dress we've put aside for you is worthy of a princess," she went on. "Would you like to see it?"

"Of course." I looked around, wondering where Sarah was.

"Come this way, please."

The woman stepped directly into the center of the maze of mirrors, and disappeared. As she did, the reflections scattered and reformed, the way they do when you toss a penny in a fountain.

I stared at my own bewildered face in the mirror, multiplied an infinite number of times. I was barefoot, and the security tag on the gorgeous beige dress was starting to chafe under my armpit.

I hope this doesn't count as shoplifting, I thought, as I followed the woman into the mirror.

"*there* you are," she said, as i emerged on the other side. We stood in the hallway of what seemed like an elegant, old-fashioned office building, with ornate moldings and doors of gleaming dark wood lining the hall. The deep green carpet was soft as velvet beneath my bare feet.

Some of the doors had engraved brass plaques on them— FREIDA'S FANTASTIC FIDDLE BOWS, the nearest one read. THE BEST IN ALL OF FAERY! I wanted to read the others, but the woman was waiting for me in the doorway directly across the hall. She shut the door behind me as I stepped inside.

The Wee Folk shop was tiny and filled with shelves of buttons and threads and bolts of fabric. There was a small, old-fashioned sewing machine and chair next to a desk. "Now," the woman said, as she led me to a tiny curtained booth behind the desk, "if you would step into the dressing room and disrobe—"

"Disrobe?" I squeezed inside, letting the curtain fall closed behind me.

"This dress has been custom-made just for you, Miss Morganne! I'm certainly not going to let you leave without a fitting." Her long arm poked through the curtain and hovered there, waiting.

Reluctantly I slipped out of the knockout beige number and draped it over the woman's arm, which she promptly withdrew.

"Marvelous," I heard her say. "Let me get rid of this old rag and bring you a *real* dress. Be right back!"

She was probably only gone for a minute, but a minute is a long time to stand barefoot in your bra and panties in a dressing room in faeryland, wondering what the fek is going to happen next. Just as I was starting to get chilly, I heard her footsteps returning.

"Here you go, Miss!" The arm poked through the curtains once more, this time proudly offering the one-of-a-kind prom dress Wee Folk Custom Tailors & Alterations had whipped up on my behalf.

"Well?" she asked. "Whaddya think?"

"It's . . . indescribable." If only it were. Imagine the kind of cheap, last-minute Cinderella costume you'd get a kid for Halloween at the drugstore. Puffy pink sleeves, layers of pink taffeta, bubblegum pink polyester bodice. It had, excuse me, bows around the waist, made of pink lace-edged ribbon and a whole lotta ugly.

"Really, my dear," the saleswoman said proudly, "you are sure to be the absolute belle of the ball in a dress like this. Unless you'd prefer something more princessy?"

"No!" I was trying not to gag. "This is plenty princessy, thanks."

"Let me know if you need help putting it on!"

Putting it on? Ugh. But since this woman had taken away the other dress and my real clothes were lying on the floor of a dressing room that was located in a different dimension of reality, it was a choice between Pretty Disgusting in Pink or standing there in my underwear. I slipped the nightmare dress over my head and stepped out from behind the curtain, keeping my eyes fixed on the floor in case there was a mirror nearby.

"Oh! *Gorgeous!*" the saleswoman twittered, as she spun me around and yanked up the zipper. "Absolutely perfect for the junior prom. Innocent, yet feminine! Glamorous, yet feminine! Classically elegant—"

"Yet feminine?" It was just a guess.

"Exactly. Tell your date to bring a white corsage. Red would clash. Yellow would clash too." The saleswoman pursed her lips. "Really, there are not very many colors you can wear with this shade of pink."

"No," I said, looking down at myself in dismay. "There aren't." The layers of stiff taffeta made my legs itch, and I found myself hopping back and forth on my bare feet like Tammy doing the Reverse Easter Bunny soccer move Colin had taught her.

Tammy would love this dress, I thought, remembering how funny she looked in her princess skirt and soccer pants. *A pair of cleats would really complete the outfit. It would be sporty, yet feminine. . . .*

And then I remembered.

Shoe equals clue.

"You're so right about the color!" I exclaimed. The woman beamed. "Do you happen to know," I asked, trying to sound casual, "where I might have some shoes dyed to match?"

"You'll need to consult the shoemaker, of course," she said. "He's very rarely in; we almost never see him. But we can try. Follow me."

We left the tailoring shop and walked down the long, green-carpeted hallway. "Sorry it's so messy," the Wee Folk woman apologized, as we turned a corner and the hallway started to curve gently. "We're terribly busy this time of year. We've made so many dresses, we have to store them in the hall!" Along one curved wall was rack after rack of formal dresses, grouped by color: red, orange, yellow, green, blue, indigo, purple. . . .

It's a rainbow, I realized. *A rainbow of prom dresses . . .*

The hallway dead-ended at a wall with a small door in it, no more than three feet high. Together we crouched down to listen. The tiny plaque read GO AWAY, NOBODY'S HOME, but through the door we could hear a *tap-tap-tapping* sound, like the sound of a tiny hammer.

"You're in luck," said the Wee Folk woman. She grunted as she straightened herself up. "It sounds like Jolly Dan Dabby is here after all."

twelve

i was so nervous about the fact that i was about to meet an actual leprechaun that I could barely bring myself to knock. I was afraid that I might frighten the shy, reclusive creature away. I shouldn't have worried.

"What!" bellowed a male voice from behind the door. He sounded plenty big in attitude, if not in actual height.

"Relax, Jolly Dan," the Wee Folk woman said. "I have a customer for you. Unless you've gone out of business?"

"Wiseass," I could have sworn I heard him say. "This customer—it's not a great looming skyscraper of a thing, like you, is it?"

"Not quite, no," the woman replied, rolling her eyes. She was a few inches taller than me. "But not a shrimp like you either."

"Humph."

The Wee Folk woman turned to me. "Don't take any nonsense from Jolly Dan," she stage-whispered. "He can be horribly rude, but it's just an act. Inside he's really very sweet."

The little door flew open. There, looking every inch a leprechaun (and there were maybe twenty-four inches of him, total), was a miniature bearded man, green coat, buckle boots, smoking a pipe, the whole deal. He looked me up and down and made a face of pure revulsion.

"Disgusting!" he roared. "That is, without question, the most hideous dress I've ever seen!"

I liked him already.

"Jolly Dan Dabby," said the woman coolly, "allow me to present the Half-Goddess Morganne." She bent down and gave a knock to the top of his hat. "She's a partial *divinity*, you shrunken oaf! She is a very *prestigious* customer."

"How do you do," I said, extending my hand down to him. He ignored it.

"By the beard of Saint Patrick, I hope you're not going to ask Jolly Dan Dabby to make shoes to match that puke-a-thon of a gown," he grumbled. "I'd rather retire right now! And I can afford to, believe you me."

"Perhaps this conversation should take place in private," the Wee Folk woman said, fanning herself with a hand. "Where it can't upset anyone's digestion."

Jolly Dan glared up at me.

I could play his game. I glared back down at him.

"Well," he said, after the staring contest got old. "Come in, then." And he disappeared back through the three-foot-high door.

What could I do? Feeling very Alice in Wonderland, I gathered up my poofy taffeta skirt, crouched down and prepared to wiggle my way through.

"Careful with the dress!" the Wee Folk woman cried in alarm.

Jolly Dan stuck his head back out. "Not that way, you 'half-goddess.'" He said it like he'd meant to say "half-wit." "Use the service entrance! Does Jolly Dan Dabby have to do *all* the thinking around here?"

It turned out the service entrance was a normal-sized door, partially hidden behind one of the dress racks in the hallway. The Wee Folk woman offered many anxious reminders to be careful with her precious pink creation, and threw in more ass-kissy compliments about how stunning I looked in it. I assured her that Jolly Dan had not altered my opinion of the dress one bit, which was the sad truth.

Then she left, and I entered the shoemaker's shop alone. Luckily the ceiling was high enough for me to stand, if I scrunched a little bit.

Jolly Dan was already back at work, alternately puffing on his pipe and *tap-tap-tapping* away on a cowboy boot that was nearly as big as he was.

"You're not really gonna wear that thing, are you?" he remarked, as he worked. "It's like—like—"

"Like Cinderella fell into a vat of Pepto-Bismol, I know," I agreed. "But it's all I have at the moment." I watched him hammer away at the boot, and wondered what would be the best way to raise the subject of Colin's enchantment. Jolly

Dan didn't seem the type who would automatically help out a tackily dressed stranger just because she'd turned up in his shop with a spell to unravel.

"Do you prefer to be called Jolly" I asked. "Or Dan? Or . . . ?"

"Jolly Dan prefers to be left alone," he snapped. "Do you need shoes or not?"

Okay, chitchat was definitely not the right approach. "I need your help," I said. "I have a friend who's been enchanted by the Faery Folk."

"A friend, or *more* than a friend?" His bushy eyebrows waggled up and down independently of each other. "You only get one chance to ask Jolly Dan for a favor, you know. Don't mess it up with half-truths, you half-goddess, you."

"He's more than a friend," I corrected myself. "He's very special to me. That's why Queen Titania enchanted him."

"Is he just a mortal, then? Or some fraction of a bigshot divinity, like you?"

"He's a mortal," I replied, though I had never thought of Colin as "just" a mortal. "He's a normal, human-type guy."

"Good luck to him, then." Jolly Dan put his pipe down, flipped the boot over and placed it on a shoe form that held it securely upside down. There was a big hole in the bottom of the boot, and he shook his head in disapproval.

"My friend's name is Colin," I went on stubbornly. I hadn't come this far to let a grouchy leprechaun blow me off. "They make him attend the faery balls every night while he's supposed to be sleeping, even though he doesn't want to. It's exhausting, and it's making him sick."

Jolly Dan snipped around the sole of the boot with a tiny

pair of scissors. Each snip seemed angrier than the last. "Jolly Dan never goes to those balls," he growled. "I don't suppose you'd care to know why?"

"Of course I would."

"Because." He ripped the worn-out sole off the boot with a single pull. "Do you know how hard it is to dance with someone more than twice your size?"

OMG, I thought. *Is that what's bugging this guy? His height?* "It's pretty difficult, I'd imagine," I said, with as much sympathy as I could muster.

"It is. It's embarrassing, is what it is. How tall is this 'special friend' of yours?"

"About six foot."

"Ha!" he exclaimed. "Jolly Dan Dabby has *no* sympathy. None. What. So. Ever."

"Mr. Dabby," I pleaded. "My friend isn't well, and it's getting worse by the day. I honestly don't know how long he can survive with so little rest." I sank down to my knees to be at eye level with the leprechaun. "I've been told that you are the only person who can help me release him from this enchantment. Is that true?"

"It is," he said, taking a fresh piece of leather from a nearby shelf. "And I suppose you want me to tell you how."

"I do."

He trimmed the leather into the proper shape as he spoke. "Well, first I'd have to know his shoe size."

"I can find that out," I said, glad to have something concrete to do.

"Not your silly numbers." He snorted. "I'd need an actual

shoe of his, one that his own foot has thoroughly broken in. A shoe that fits him—"

"Like a glove?" I finished eagerly.

"No, semi-goddess-girl, like a shoe! Gloves go on the hands." He shook his head at my stupidity. "Once I've got a shoe that's molded to his foot, I fashion a form from it. Then I make him a brand new pair." He took a puff on his pipe and smiled. "Lovely dancing shoes. Ones that have a little magic in them."

"Then—what?"

"Then he has to put them on, you genius! Not on these!" He wiggled his fingers in my face. "On his feet! One spin around the dance floor wearing my shoes, and the enchantment's broken. He'll be your own overgrown, 'normal, human-type guy' once more. Sounds like a real loser if you ask me." He made a gagging gesture with his finger.

I ignored the loser comment. "Does that mean the faeries won't bother him again?" I asked, thinking of Mike Fitch and every other boy I might conceivably meet in my life. "Or will they find other mortals to take his place?"

He chuckled darkly. "They wouldn't dare, believe me. All those hard-partying Faery Folk come to me for their dancing shoes. If they cross me even once, I'll make 'em so their toes pinch and their feet blister." He took out a second small hammer and, now using both hands, doubled his efforts tapping in the new sole of the boot.

So all I need to save Colin is a pair of magic shoes made by a leprechaun? I thought. *Piece of cake!* "Well," I said, feeling relieved. "This won't be too difficult, then!"

"Not for you, chickie," Jolly Dan said. "I'm the one that has to make the shoes. *If* we can work out a deal, of course."

"Of course," I said quickly. "May I ask how much they'll cost?"

"Jolly Dan has plenty of money." His two-hammered tapping on the bottom of the boot was starting to take on familiar rhythms. It reminded me of Dylan's signature drum riff from "Rock and Roll All Nite," but a lot of those heavy metal drum parts sounded alike to me, frankly. "Jolly Dan Dabby only makes shoes that he *wants* to make," the leprechaun added, with an air of mystery.

I could tell this half-pint grump wanted something, but what was it? He wasn't making it easy to find out. "Will you do it to help Colin, then?"

His face reddened with anger. "I should knock myself out bringing more happiness to a six-foot lunk who's already got a half-goddess girlfriend?" The redder he turned, the louder he got. "What about *me*? What about Jolly *Dan's* needs?"

Hmmm, I thought. *It's never a good sign when you talk about yourself in the third person.* "I think I get it," I said. "You want to be the apple of someone's eye, don't you?"

He looked startled, as if he might say something, but then he turned back to his work. I watched him in silence.

"I'll help you on one condition," he muttered at last.

"Whatever it is, I'll—"

"Don't be so hasty! What I'm going to ask you to do isn't easy. In fact, it's probably impossible. *Very* probably."

Definitely impossible might be an obstacle, but very probably impossible were odds I thought I could handle. I listened.

"I'll make your boring, ordinary human-guy the shoes,"

he said slowly, "*if* you find me a date for the Spring Faery Ball. A *real* date," he added. "Someone like me. Not a giant klutz of a girl. No offense."

"That'll be a cinch," I said, giddy with relief. "Fixing up a charming and attractive gentleman like you?"

"You forgot prosperous." Then he looked embarrassed. "Even so, it's not going to be as easy as you think."

"Why not?"

"Because," he said, giving me a *don't they teach you giant klutzes anything at school?* look. "There are no female leprechauns. Didn't you know that? Duh."

That piece-of-cake feeling disappeared like a wisp of smoke from Jolly Dan's pipe. "Duh," I echoed stupidly. "I forgot about that." My mind turned over the possibilities. "Does it have to be a girl?" I asked, after a moment. "I'm just checking."

Jolly Dan gave a sad shrug. "Yup. Sorry, but that's the way I swing. It's a frustrating situation, to say the least." He lifted the resoled boot off the form and examined it. "Look," he said with a sniff. "Even these smelly things come in pairs. Now, if you don't mind, I have work to do."

"I'll find you someone," I said, as touched by his loneliness as I was determined to help Colin. "Get yourself a tux and practice your dance moves. I'll be back."

"Yeah, right," he scoffed. His voice was gruff, but I could have sworn I saw him quickly wipe away a tear. "See ya 'round, tall stuff."

i left jolly dan's shop the same way i came in, through the service door that, from the inside, was marked with a plaque reading GIANT KLUTZES EXIT HERE. And I managed to wheedle the beautiful beige dress back from the Wee Folk woman by asking her to store the pink gown for me until prom.

"I don't want to get it dirty," I explained. "My sister likes to play dress up with my clothes."

"I completely understand," she said grandly. "We'll take excellent care of it. Are you and Mr. Dabby all set about the shoes?"

Naturally I hadn't bothered to ask Jolly Dan Dabby about pink shoes, but it's not like I was going to be needing them. I had no intention of putting that pink dress on ever again.

"I think Jolly Dan understands exactly what I want," I told her. "But now I have to go. Would you mind showing me back to the—the, uh—"

"The elevator? Of course."

I followed her back into the hallway. The elevator was small, with a folding iron gate across the door. With a strong pull she yanked the gate open and held it while I stepped inside. The interior was completely mirrored, even the ceiling.

"Relax and pamper yourself," she called, pulling the gate shut with a clang. "Get a manicure! A facial! A massage! You only get to go to your junior prom once!"

I pressed the button that read STROHMAN'S DRESSING ROOM (the other one read HARRODS) and the elevator lurched into motion, though whether it was going up, down or sideways I couldn't say.

thirteen

Moments later I was back in Strohman's, standing in front of the angled mirrors and the kaleidoscope of reflections within them. Looming over the right shoulder of each of an endless number of Morgans were an equal number of Sarahs, wearing facial expressions that were infinitely more impatient than a single Sarah could ever manage on her own.

"So?" she asked, as if for the gazillionth time. "You're gonna take it, right?"

"Take what?" I was still thinking about the cool way the elevator had morphed into the dressing room mirrors in Strohman's the instant the doors slid open.

"The *dress,* Morgan! You're standing there like you're mesmerized or something. Did you even check the price?"

I hadn't, of course. I twisted around to see the tag, but it kept jumping out of reach as I moved. Sarah rolled her eyes and grabbed it.

"Hold still for a minute—oh my God! It's on *sale!*" To Sarah, this was the ultimate sign from above. "That settles it. I'm putting this dress on layaway for you."

"Sarah, I know you're trying to help," I said, turning around so she could unzip me. "And I appreciate it. But there's some really important stuff I need to figure out first—"

"Morgan." Sarah spun me around again and grabbed me by both shoulders. "Six words! Junior prom. Gorgeous dress. Mike Fitch. Whatever else you need to figure out can't be that big a deal."

That's because you never had to play matchmaker for a leprechaun, I thought, as I went to change.

by the time i got home from the mall, the front yard and rear garden of my house were overrun with garden gnomes. Near the mailbox: two gnomes in sun hats having a tea party. Clustered around the birdbath: four gnomes smoking cigars and playing cards. Gnomes peeked out mischievously from behind the trash cans, sunbathed on the lawn and played hide-and-seek in the shrubs. Dad had truly outdone himself this year.

I stood on the driveway with my keys in my hand, taking it all in. *Mom must be gearing up for a major tantrum,* I thought. *This is gonna be interesting.*

But then I heard her voice, coming from the side of the house. She wasn't having a tantrum. In fact, she sounded pleased.

"How about this one?" she was saying. "Look how cute it is, in its little dress!"

"It's not important what the wee bugger looks like. I just need to whack the limbs off it."

Colin and my mother rounded the side of the house. I just stared at them.

"Good afternoon, Mor," Colin said cheerfully. "Did ye manage all yer shopping? Yer ma told me there's a big dance comin' up at school. Ye never mentioned."

What's Colin doing here? I thought. *And why the fek is my mother telling him about my prom?*

"Why do you want to whack the limbs off a gnome?" I asked.

"Colin has the *most* prize-winning idea for his robot." Mom sounded giddy. "Instead of some boring, mechanical-looking thing, he wants to conceal the robotics inside a, um—what did you call it, Colin?"

"An anthropomorphic casing. One of these garden gnomes, basically," he explained. "Morgan, ye saved me arse—pardon, ma'am—by bringing the binder over this morning. Once I showed Alice me notes and sketches she was convinced. I skedaddled over to take some measurements, but yer ma has kindly offered to sacrifice one in the name of science."

My mom just smiled.

"They're just the right size, and you have to admit, the aes-thetics are bound to attract attention," Colin went on. "Could be the competitive edge we need to win this bloody contest."

"And they're not valuable *at all,* so there's no harm in de-stroying one!" Mom said happily. "Or more than one! Are you sure you don't need several, Colin? We have so many."

This was, without question, the most evil and devious

thing I'd ever seen my mom do. It was both terrifying and totally impressive.

"Did you guys ask Dad about this?" I said.

"Your father took Tammy to her soccer game," Mom said quickly. "They won't be back for an hour, at least. And Colin's on a tight schedule. Very tight! He has a competition to prepare for!"

"Of course, maybe I should ask yer husband before I take one." Colin looked alarmed. "I didn't realize—"

"That my mom is trying to pull a fast one?" I cracked.

"A few gnomes more or less, your father won't even notice." Mom hoisted up one of the tea party gnomes and pushed it into Colin's arms. "There's no need to hang around waiting for Daniel; you must have *so* much work to do back at school!"

She stalked the lawn like the Grim Reaper of Gnomes. "Hmm! That one would be perfect!" She pounced on a card-playing gnome and lifted it by the arm. Its cigar slipped out of its mouth and landed on the grass. "It has a lot of personality, don't you think?"

Colin looked at me helplessly, but Mom sounded more energized by the minute. "Why not take a bunch of them, chop them all up and see which one works best?" she suggested ruthlessly. Then she checked her watch. "If we go soon I can drive you back to the dorm instead of you waiting for the bus; this way you can take as many as you want—"

If my dad hadn't pulled up that minute, I'm sure my mom would have found a reason to pack every single one of the gnomes into her Mini Cooper, even if it meant lashing them to the roof. As soon as the Subaru was parked Tammy jumped out, dressed in her soccer uniform and shin guards, with twelve sparkly barrettes in her hair. Dad followed, suspicion evident on his face as soon as he saw us standing in the yard.

"Over so soon?" Mom exclaimed, in her most innocent, *no, I'm not in the middle of slaughtering your precious gnome collection* voice.

"Half the kids on the other team had stomach flu," Dad said flatly. "We rescheduled. What—what are you doing?" The card-playing gnome still dangled from Mom's hand. Its painted-on smile looked increasingly like a grimace of pain.

"Why is Colin stealing the gnome?" Tammy asked, gazing up at him with big wounded eyes. Colin dropped the tea-party gnome onto the grass like a hot potato.

"He's going to make a robot out of it, dear!" Mom shoved another gnome into Colin's now-empty arms. "Won't that be interesting?"

The ice-cream-melting-in-the-sun way Tammy's face went slack with horror was a thing to behold. "Noooooooo!" she screeched. "You'll *kill* it!"

"Oh, dear," Colin said, taking a giant step back. "I'd never hurt yer gnomies, luv. Sorry for causing all the ruckus, dear people. I'd best head over to the garden shop at Lucky Lou's and see if they have any left."

"Don't be ridiculous, Colin; you shouldn't waste your money when we have so many *extra*," Mom declared. "Daniel, surely you can spare one of these things for Colin's robot project? After all he's done for Tammy?"

"He's going to *kill* it!" Tammy screamed.

Dad was looking fairly robotic himself at this point. His

face was completely expressionless in a way that spelled nothing but trouble. The way I saw it, he had two options—he could read Mom the riot act in front of everyone or he could try to reason with a hysterical kid who was starting to hyperventilate. Neither task would be pleasant; which would he choose?

"You can't kill a garden gnome, Tammy," he said finally. "They're not alive."

"Maybe they are," Tammy said stubbornly.

Staying heroically in control of his temper, Dad picked up the partner of the card-playing gnome that Colin was now holding and rapped it on the head. "Look, Tammy. It's made of plaster." He knocked on the others. "This one's—ouch!—concrete. This one's fiberglass. This one's, I don't know"—he turned it over—"'Made in China.' It's molded plastic, or whatever they make things out of in China." He knelt down to Tammy's level. "See? They're not real."

"But maybe they are!" Tammy countered, completely unimpressed by Dad's logic. "Maybe gnomes are missological! Maybe they're controversial! Ask Morgan, she knows about stuff like that."

I was doing my absolute best to keep out of this, and when all eyes turned to me I was off to one side of the yard, gazing deeply into an azalea bush. It was just coming into bright pink bud, and nestled below its low branches were two gnomes I didn't recall ever seeing before—not in the garage, or on the lawn, or anywhere.

One was wearing a fancy party dress, the same vivid pink as the azalea buds. The other was wearing—could it be? I blinked hard. Twice. But there it was.

Who ever heard of a garden gnome dressed in a tuxedo?

"Tell them, Morgan!" Tammy demanded. "Are gnomes real or not?"

They'd better be real, I thought, fighting my urge to jump up and down and yell, "Yessss!" with my fists pumping in the air. *Because the plastic chick in the pink dress would make one heck of a prom date for a leprechaun.*

A complex negotiation followed, with tammy acting as the Holy Protector of the Gnome People, and my mom acting sickly sweet so as to diffuse the impending Wrath of Dad, and Dad acting like his wrath was being held back only by his desire not to have a stroke in front of poor Colin, who was now trapped in an episode of *When Rawlinsons Attack: A Nice Connecticut Family Goes Bad*, with no commercial break in sight.

Finally Colin was permitted to leave, with a single gnome wrapped in newspaper ("So it won't get chilly," Tammy insisted), which he swore to use only to make a papier-mâché cast for his robot project, and which he would return unharmed.

"Make sure it can breathe!" Tammy begged.

"It can't breathe because it's not alive—oh, never mind." Dad looked like he needed to lie down. Mom had already made a quick escape to the kitchen, where she was no doubt busy whipping up Dad's favorite dessert, in case charm, denial and general diversionary tactics weren't enough to save her marriage.

Tammy's voice receded into a singsong background

whine as I walked Colin to the bus stop (he'd firmly refused a ride from each of my parents—who'd want to spend another minute with any of us, if he could help it?). "Papier mâché," he grumbled. "I'm not much of a hand with the arts and crafts. D'ye think Lucky Lou's has any more of the wee gnome buggers? I think I'd do better to buy one."

"You know, Colin," I said, trying to sound adorably sentimental and not like an idiot, "I'd kinda prefer you didn't chop one up either. Just, you know—in case."

"What? In case they're alive?" Colin almost dropped the newspaper bundle.

"Careful!" I said, leaping to catch it. "No, of course not. It would just be sad to see one gutted and turned into a robot. Like having the family dog stuffed."

"Ye don't have a dog, ye daft thing." Colin yawned and rubbed his eyes. "Never mind, then. I don't want to upset anyone's delicate sensibilities. I'll do the papier-mâché job and paint it. It'll look like a proper freak of nature, though, that I can promise ye."

He didn't mention it, but I could tell the slight uphill walk to the bus stop had been a struggle for him. He was breathing hard and looked paler with each step. I said I'd wait until the bus came, and we sat together on the bench. His head fell on my shoulder at once, and though my back was twisted painfully out of shape with his dead weight leaning against me, I hoped the bus would be late so he could get an extra minute or two of rest.

As he napped, I scoped out the pair of beat-up Nikes on his feet and remembered my instructions. *Soon,* I thought, *those stinky sneakers will be mine.*

fourteen

My mission was clear: Short stuff in a dress was what Jolly Dan wanted, and short stuff in a dress was what he was going to get. All I had to do was convince the gnome.

This would be so much easier if you guys were still in the garage, I thought, late that night, as I snuck across the yard with a flashlight from the kitchen junk drawer. Professional closet declutterers like my mom shouldn't even have junk drawers, it occurred to me, but they probably shouldn't have lawns full of tacky garden ornaments either.

It was almost midnight. Tammy had been asleep for hours. Normally my parents would be in bed too by this time, but from inside the house floated the melodic rise and fall of their argument.

They sounded thoroughly distracted, but even so, I tried my best to not make a sound or let the beam of my flashlight hit any windows. I didn't think any of our neighbors kept guns at home, but if they did, the tragic and embarrassing headline pretty much wrote itself: "Teen Girl Mistaken for Intruder, Shot in Own Yard While Attempting to Converse with Garden Gnomes." Not the legacy I was planning to leave.

In daylight the gnomes looked fake and foolish, but in the dark they seemed different, more natural, like they were actually part of the landscape. Every time my flashlight beam found one nestled in the grass or under a shrub it startled me. But they didn't move, even when I let the light linger, searching for some sign of life.

How am I going to get them to talk to me? I wondered.

Try saying hello, a little voice inside me suggested.

But they're gnomes, I argued with myself.

And you're a half-goddess, so start acting like one! my inner voice argued back. *You think you need a guy in a chicken suit to do your magic for you? Grow up, already!*

Okay, fine. Maybe I just needed some confidence. I'd already decided that my first attempt at matchmaking would be with the gnome girl in the pink dress. If she said no—this was assuming I could communicate with her at all—I'd work my way through every girl gnome in the yard. Potentially it could be a long night. I skulked along the grass to the azalea bush, and peeked inside.

There she was, with her tuxedoed pal, frozen in a festive, party pose. Mid-dance, mid-flirt, mid-"can I get you a drink?"—who knew what these two were in the middle of? It suddenly seemed kind of awkward to try to set her up with someone else while her date was standing right there.

"Excuse me," I said, picking up the tuxedoed gnome and

moving him to another shrub. He seemed a bit out of place next to the two pointy-hatted, red-cheeked gnomes with their long gray beards and frothy mugs of ale, but I figured it was only temporary. "Hang out with the guys for a minute, would you?" I said, in case he was listening. "Pretend your date and I are going to the ladies' room together."

I returned to the azalea. Was it my imagination, or was there a look of relief on the gnome girl's face? Did the pink painted-on folds of her dress ripple ever so slightly in the night breeze? I shivered and crossed my arms for warmth.

"Stylish friend you've got there," I said. "Do you mind me asking if it's serious?"

No answer.

"That's a pretty dress," I tried. "How did you ever find shoes to match?"

No answer.

"I don't suppose you'd be interested in being fixed up with a leprechaun?" I asked in desperation. No answer. I turned and surveyed the dark lawn with my flashlight. *Maybe I'll have better luck with a gnome chick who's not already hooked up,* I thought. Then I heard a rustling noise behind me.

"A leprechaun?" The voice was high and grainy, like an adult's voice that had been sped up to munchkin pitch. "You're kidding! I always thought they were mythological."

Slowly I turned around. Miss Party Pink Gnome Thing was applying a fresh coat of lip gloss. "Thanks for getting rid of that guy who was hitting on me, by the way," she added, as she smacked her lips together. "His Frodo impersonation was getting really old."

"No problem," I said, trying to stay calm while thinking,

I'm talking with one of my dad's garden gnomes; how cool is that?

"He said his name is Tux. Can you stand it?" she said. "Guys and their pickup lines. I'm Glendryn," she added, checking her teeth in a tiny compact mirror.

"Nice to meet you, Glendryn. I'm Mor—"

"The half-goddess Morganne, I know! Everyone knows who *you* are!" She laughed and tucked the mirror back into her sparkly pink purse, which was no bigger than an iPod pouch. "Though not everyone believes *you're* real either! I can't wait to tell my sister I met you."

"Wow, that's awesome," I said. Who knew I was a celebrity in gnome world? "Which one is your sister? Is she here in the yard?"

Glendryn's expression changed to one of pure misery. "Drenwyn is gathering berries from a bush that's like, twenty feet away." Her lip started to quiver. "We've never been separated before. It's really upsetting."

"You must be, uh, very close." I wasn't sure what else to say. Twenty feet was still pretty close, in my opinion, but then again I wasn't two feet tall.

"Of course we're close. We're twins! All gnomes are twins, didn't you know that? Except for"—she paused for a moment—"the Occasional Exceptions, I guess. But *practically* all of us are twins. I certainly am! And my sister and I always, always do everything together."

Uh-oh, that inner voice of mine cautioned. *Leprechauns do everything alone, and gnomes do everything together.* But surely they could get through one date, right?

"Listen, Glendryn," I said. "If you want, I can bring your

sister Drenwyn over here to be with you, and put Tux and his Frodo act over by the raspberry bush. I'm sure no one will notice."

Glendryn's gnomishly crinkled face crinkled up even more. "Could you? Oh, Morganne! Everything they say about you is true!"

As amusing as it would be to know what all the gnomes were saying about me, I thought it best to press on. "Okay, but I need you to do me a favor too," I said. "I have this friend who needs a date for a very special event. It's the Spring Faery Ball."

"I always *wanted* to go to that!" Glendryn clapped her hands together. They made a little *clunk*, like the sound of plastic hitting plastic.

"Excellent! He's a really nice guy and I'm sure you'd have a great time." I gestured at her bubblegum-pink princess outfit. "And you already have the dress."

"This old thing? No, I will definitely need something new. What to wear, what to wear! And he's a leprechaun, you say? How exotic! We'll have to meet first, of course. A proper introduction is required, absolutely required." She peered up at me. "Sometimes people assume that just because a girl is a gnome, you don't have to treat her like a lady. That is *so* wrong!"

"I can take you to meet him this week." I pictured myself with Glendryn tucked under my arm like a football as I sprinted through the mirror in Strohman's dressing room.

"First, I have a few questions." Glendryn fluffed her pink skirt flirtatiously. "What's his name?"

"Jolly Dan Dabby."

"Profession?"

"Shoemaker."

"Height?"

I held my hand at knee level. "About this tall. Just right for you."

"Perfect!" she squealed. "Good dresser?"

I thought of Jolly Dan's buckled boots and funky green leprechaun hat. "He's traditional in style, I would say. He definitely has his own look."

"Fine, fine." She nodded approvingly. "Now, of course it's not the most important thing; the most important thing is character! And personality! And what lives inside a person's heart! But tell me the truth: Is he good with money?"

"The best," I said confidently. "Very hardworking and fiscally sound, from what I hear."

Glendryn twirled in delight and then curtsied. "It would be my pleasure to make his acquaintance, then. And he has to take my sister too, of course!"

Some noisy night insect buzzed right past my ear as Glendryn was talking; I wasn't sure I'd heard her right. "Sorry, Glendryn, what was the last thing you said?"

"I said, he has to take my sister too." She beamed. "We do *everything* together."

talk about feast or famine, i thought, sneaking across the lawn once more with the gnome named Tux under my arm. *Jolly Dan's first date ever, and it's gonna be with twins.*

It took me a minute to find Drenwyn in the dark, half-concealed among the raspberry bushes. Not surprisingly, she was a dead ringer for Glendryn, but dressed in a checked gingham frock and lace-up boots. She wore a bonnet on her head and carried a small wicker basket for the berries.

Stamped from the same mold, I couldn't help thinking, but then I wondered if that was rude.

There was another girl gnome in the berry patch with Drenwyn. She was similarly dressed, but with a cranky expression on her face. Most of the gnomes had bright-eyed, round-cheeked faces that exuded perpetual enthusiasm. This one had more of a shrunken apple look.

When I explained to Drenwyn why I was there, she wept with joy at the prospect of being reunited with her sister. The cranky gnome girl's face puckered even more, but she said nothing and kept picking berries. Raspberries wouldn't be in season until late in summer, but each time she reached for one a berry seemed to appear just in time to get plucked and tossed in the basket. She never looked at the basket, I noticed, but she never missed. Like a mini-Sarah. Definitely UConn material, if they started drafting two-foot-high forwards.

This Tux fellow was hardly dressed for harvesting fruit, but once I helped him take off his tiny cufflinks and roll up his crisp white sleeves, he got to work without complaint. After Glendryn's comment about treating gnome girls like ladies, I figured I should try to introduce him to the cranky, apple-faced girl before I left them alone together in the berry bush. She seemed terribly shy and could barely say her name.

"Tammy," was what I thought she said.

"Small world. My sister's name is Tammy too," I offered, in an attempt to bond.

"Taffy!" she yelped. "Like the stuff that breaks your teeth!

And don't brag about your 'sister' to me. That's *so mean!*"
Then she started to cry.

Yikes, I must've said the wrong thing, I thought. I turned to
Tux and Drenwyn for help. Tux gestured for me to bend
down so he could whisper in my ear.

"She doesn't have a sister," he said.

"But I thought all gnomes were twins—"

"Practically all," he said. "Except for Taffy. She's an OE."

"A what?"

"Occasional Exception," he explained. "She's very sensitive
about it too. Don't worry, I'll cheer her up. Hey, Taffy!" he
said jovially. "Have you seen my Frodo impersonation? 'No,
Samwise, go back to the Shire! I must bear . . . this burden . . .
alone!'"

It wasn't a great impression, but he was definitely the right
height for it. And it succeeded in distracting Taffy, though
not in a good way.

"That's so *stupid,*" I heard her wail between sobs, as I carried Drenwyn back to the azalea bush to be with her sister.
"Everybody knows that hobbits . . . aren't . . . real. . . ."

fifteen

With only ten days left before the junior prom, this is how things stood: I had a guy I was crazy about who couldn't take me to prom because he was leaving the country (if he didn't end up in the hospital first), another guy who wanted to take me but I wouldn't let him, a pair of stinky sneakers to steal, a fabulous dress on layaway, and a crabby leprechaun who had to be convinced to escort a pair of excitable plastic gnome sisters to the Spring Faery Ball.

I can so totally make this work, I thought, as I rode up the mall escalators to Strohman's. It was Monday, after school, and I was going use all my powers of persuasion to get Jolly Dan Dabby to say yes to not one, but two dates for the Faery Ball.

Or, if that didn't work, who knows? Maybe he had a friend.

* * *

"I don't have 'a friend,' you nitwit! I'm a leprechaun! We're known to be solitary! We hate to mingle! We're seen in public so rarely that half the Faery Folk don't even believe we exist!"

Jolly Dan was not reacting positively to the twin concept.

"Listen." I took a deep breath, which made me notice how strongly Jolly Dan's shop smelled of feet. "First of all, it was your idea to go to the Faery Ball, so don't give me that solitary leprechaun routine. You're not solitary. You're lonely."

"Humph," he said.

"Second of all, these sisters are perfectly nice girls and they want to go with you. I've done my part. Go or don't go, I don't care, but you still have to make the magic shoes for Colin." I stood up too fast and bumped my head on the ceiling. "A deal's a deal."

"Don't try to bamboozle me, you double-height half-goddess!" he retorted. "I said find me a date. You found me *two* dates. No deal!"

I stared at him.

He stared at me.

I stared at him harder. I had never, ever lost a staring contest in my life, and believe me, Tammy had given me tons of practice.

"You know," he finally said, looking away in discomfort, "I do have a customer who came in to get his shoes resoled for the ball." Jolly Dan grabbed his hammers and a pair of Manolo Blahniks from the shelf. "He was complaining about not knowing who to ask."

"Perfect," I said. "A double date. You'll win extra points

for customer service, the sisters will be happy and I'll get my shoes for Colin."

"Not so fast," he warned. "This guy's an elf. He's very—" Jolly Dan held his hand in the air, as high as he could reach.

"Tall?"

"Grotesquely so." Jolly Dan cringed. "Even bigger than you." He turned away from me and started drumming with his hammers. "The ladies might find him repulsive."

Would they? The word elf just made me think of Orlando Bloom. Sarah was still secretly obsessed with him; she used to keep his picture taped to the inside of her locker before she started dating Dylan. Surely no one could object to being set up with a hottie like that?

"It's what's on the inside of a person that counts," I said to Jolly Dan. "That's what one of the 'ladies' told me." I didn't bother to mention that she'd also inquired about his finances.

"Come back tomorrow," Jolly Dan muttered, as he began *tap-tap-tapping* away on the Manolos. "I'll tell you what the elf says then."

Glendryn and Drenwyn loved the idea of double-dating, "as long as we stay together the *whole* time," they said. And the elf concept prompted fits of giggles.

Meanwhile, matchmaker me was feeling pretty wiped out from my middle-of-the-night gnome visits, and this got me even more worried about how long Colin would be able to last with only fitful half-sleep and catnaps to keep him going.

During my first free period at school on Tuesday, I went to the library and looked up "Sleep Deprivation":

> Sleep Deprivation has been used as a means of torture in numerous military conflicts and also as an aid to interrogation. . . . In experiments, rats forced to endure prolonged sleep deprivation exhibited disoriented behavior, weight loss and eventually death. . . .

Death? *This double date* will *happen,* I thought. *There's a lot more at stake here than Jolly Dan's love life.* Or mine, for that matter. Now that I was trying to avoid having any fleeting urges of lust for my male classmates, boys were pretty much all I could think about. I tried to imagine them the way they were in middle school, when they were a head shorter than me with braces and zits and squeaky voices, but the more I tried to downplay their cuteness the yummier they seemed. Changing classes was the worst, with all those boy bodies rushing by, smelling of soap and aftershave—it was like I was trapped in the Hotties of East Norwich High School pinup calendar.

To keep me on track, and also because I was really freaked out about the sleep-deprived rats, I ran into the girl's bathroom between classes, snuck out my cell phone and called Colin to see how he was feeling. He didn't pick up.

Probably busy in the lab, I thought, trying not to panic. *I'll call him again later.*

After school I took the bus straight to the mall to see Jolly Dan. The sales staff at Strohman's were starting to recognize me. I didn't want them to think I was a total klepto or they'd never let me back in the store, so I visited the beige dress at the layaway counter for a while before heading into the dressing room.

"Why don't you just buy it?" the clerk said, taking it down off the rack for me to look at. "It's the nicest dress in the store, but for some weird reason it didn't fit anyone until you tried it on."

"That *is* weird," I said, forcing myself to sound surprised. "I probably will. I'm, uh, just not sure I can afford it."

She shoved the price tag in front of my face. It read:

> Suggested retail price $875
> Now only *$4.93!*
> You save—oops, the math is too hard but you
> rilly save a hole lot!

"This has to be a mistake," I said.

The clerk waved the tag though the barcode scanner and looked at the display on her cash register.

"It has to be, but it isn't," she said, amazed. "Miss, you are taking this dress *today* if I have to pay for it myself. I never heard of this designer either. 'Goddesswear by the Fabulous Finnbar'?"

With my stunning five-dollar prom dress purchased and neatly folded in a Strohman's bag, I ducked into the dressing room and mirror-hopped my way to Jolly Dan's. I was careful to avoid being seen by the Wee Folk woman as I made my way down the hall. I didn't have the time or the patience to admire that gag-inducing, yet feminine pink dress one more time.

"The elf is game," Jolly Dan told me, sounding wary. "But he wants to meet both sisters first."

"Fine." I was determined. "The sooner the better. I'll bring them tomorrow."

"N-not tomorrow," Jolly Dan stammered. "Tomorrow's bad. Tomorrow's busy, a very busy day. Thursday too, it's awful, I'm completely booked."

"When, then?" I demanded. "I need those shoes for my friend, as soon as possible." I fixed him with my semi-goddess stare again. "Surely you don't mean to go back on your word?"

"Hush, you demanding beanpole! It's just that . . . well, I want to spruce myself up first." All of a sudden he looked bashful—or, considering his size, make that Bashful, as in Bashful, Dopey, Sneezy, Sleepy, Doc, and the other two Disney dwarfs whose names I could never remember when Tammy quizzed me. "Nothing major," Jolly Dan mumbled, staring at the floor. "Beard trim, haircut, a new apron, lose a few pounds. You only get to make a first impression once."

What? Colin's health and maybe even his life were in danger and I had to deal with Jolly Dan's insecurity attack? "Relax! You're perfectly fine the way you are," I told him, trying not to sound impatient.

"Then why do they sell all that beauty stuff in the mall?" he asked.

It was a valid question, but I didn't have a good answer for it, so I reassured him as best I could and left. And, speaking of the mall, since I was already there I decided to buy a pair of shoes. Not for myself — for Colin. Knowing him, he almost certainly hadn't packed any extra footwear for his trip to the States. Before I could steal his old Nikes I'd have to replace them with something else, or he'd be traveling back to Ireland in his soccer cleats.

That meant I needed his shoe size, so I called him again as I rode the escalator up one more level to where the SportShoe store was. The phone rang a bunch of times before he picked up.

"Sorry, Mor, I almost missed ye there." He sounded out of breath.

"Why? Are you okay?" I thought of the dead rats and started to freak out. "Are you disoriented? Have you been losing weight?"

"Perhaps, I dunno. At the moment I'm up to me elbows in this papier-mâché gunk. Yer gnome chum is looking rather mummylike at the moment. But don't worry, I didn't cover his nose."

"That's good." I was on level three now, not far from the shoe store. "Quick question: What size shoes do you wear?"

"Same size as me feet," he quipped. "Why d'ye ask?"

"It's for a math project." Sadly, the continual making up of lame excuses was turning out to be my main semi-goddess superpower. "We're collecting the shoe sizes of people we know, and compiling statistical data and calculating the, uh, probability that two people chosen at random could, you know, share shoes and stuff." My cheeks were turning pink from lying, and I was glad he couldn't see me. "Just — what is it?"

"Ten and a half Irish, forty-five Euro, no clue what that is in American," Colin said. "A maths project, eh? That's impressive. By the time ye graduate ye'll be able to calculate the odds on the football betting pools. A useful life skill if ever there was one."

"I'll figure it out, great." Now I was standing directly outside SportShoe, with all those huge guy-sized sneakers displayed in the window, each one practically big enough to drive. "Thanks. Okay, I'll see you—"

"Hey," he said. "If ye have a sec, Mor, I wanted to talk to ye about this school dance thing yer mother mentioned—"

"Not right now, Colin. I really have to get this math assignment done." *Why why why* did my mother have to blab personal things about me to everyone she met? Especially Colin? A person with whom she should not be having conversations *at all,* in my opinion, and especially not about me?

"I just had one thing to say about it—"

"Oops," I said, cutting him off. "Can't hear you, sorry! I'm going through a tunnel—"

"A tunnel? Are ye in a train?"

"Right, I'm getting in an elevator! Later!"

I hung up on him.

Fek. Why did Colin want to talk to me about the junior prom?

He wasn't going to ask me to go with him, because he was flying back to Ireland on Sunday. Prom wasn't until Thursday. The twentieth. My birthday.

And he wasn't going to tell me *not* to go—to wait until I was older and we were both on the same continent and could attend such important and romantic life events together, the way we were obviously meant to.

Nope. I knew Colin well enough to predict exactly what he was going to say.

He was going to tell me—

Never mind. I put the whole prom thing out of my mind and went into the shoe store. The important thing was not whether or not I got to go to a stupid dance.

The important thing was that Colin got to *stop* going.

Sarah had arranged for Wednesday's final prom committee meeting to be held at Dylan's house, at the exact same time Ass Your Kiss Goodbye was not-so-coincidentally rehearsing in the garage. Sarah had also arranged for many of their friends to be randomly passing by the house. In a series of Oscar-worthy performances, each of them acted completely surprised when they saw the guys setting up, and then stuck around to listen.

Soon the rehearsal had sneakily turned into an impromptu performance, with about thirty people preparing to get their groove on in the driveway. Clem and Deirdre were giving out glow sticks, just to add to the concert atmosphere.

"Sorry about the noise," Sarah said cheerily to Mrs. Blainsvoort. All the living room windows were open, and the sounds of electric guitars being tuned and Dylan warming up on his drum kit were flooding into the house.

"Perhaps we should reschedule." Mrs. Blainsvoort looked miffed. "Or meet at your house, as we usually do?"

"No time, the prom is next week," Sarah said. "And who knew my parents were going to have our whole house painted today? Wish they'd told me earlier!" She smiled sweetly at Mrs. Blainsvoort.

"It just seems rather odd," Mrs. Blainsvoort said with suspicion, "since our only remaining agenda item is—"

"The music!" Sarah grinned. "I know!"

As the band launched into its first number, Mrs. Blainsvoort's hands flew halfway up to her ears. But instead of their usual hardcore covers of classic Kiss, today the band was trying out some mellower song stylings.

The crowd reacted with coached enthusiasm to the band's new sound. More importantly, Mrs. Blainsvoort was sucked right in.

"Oh! I *love* Abba!" she exclaimed.

"Cool! We do too!" said Sarah. The three of us—Sarah, me and Mrs. Blainsvoort—looked out the window. Under the leadership of Clem and Deirdre, the crowd in the driveway was singing along happily and waving their glow sticks in the air. It was like a light beer commercial, only more fake.

"I must say, when you first mentioned your boyfriend's band, I was expecting something—edgier," Mrs. Blainsvoort said, her hips swaying to the music. "Do they know 'Dancing Queen'?"

"If you let them play at the junior prom next week, I promise you, they will learn it," Sarah declared.

"I had no idea this was the type of music you kids are into. Perhaps I *should* reconsider." Mrs. Blainsvoort was snapping her fingers, only slightly off the beat. "I'll think about it."

The band formerly known as Ass Your Kiss Goodbye (Sarah told Mrs. Blainsvoort that they were called The Schoolboys) kept up the easy listening act until Mrs. Blainsvoort left. Then everyone came inside and a victory-is-nearly-ours toast of Red Bull was poured for all. I did my best to avoid being alone with Mike Fitch, but he snuck up on me while I was in the kitchen getting ice from the dispenser.

"So," he said, while my back was to him. "I hear you have a boyfriend who lives in Europe."

I was so startled I spun around without letting go of the switch on the refrigerator door.

"What?" A stream of ice chunks clunked and slid all over the kitchen floor. "Who? I mean, who told you that?"

He smiled and bent down to gather up the slippery wet shards.

"Sorry to startle you," he said. "It's just getting to be kind of dumb, the way I talk to Dylan and Dylan talks to Sarah and Sarah talks to you. I thought it would be better if we talked to each other. Radical, right?"

"Very," I said, holding a rapidly melting ice cube in my hand. "What do you want to talk about?" I instantly regretted asking, since I already had a good idea of what Mike wanted to talk about. "Hey, the band sounded totally convincing," I babbled, to keep him from speaking. "Even playing Muzak, you guys rock."

"Maybe we should change our name to the Ironicks," he joked. "Morgan, listen—"

"Ha ha ha." I forced myself to laugh. "Ironicks, that's pretty funny. That's really—"

"I was going to ask you to prom." He held up his hands, as if to show me he wasn't carrying a weapon. "Not as a date.

If your heart belongs to someone, I totally respect that. But if the lucky Euro-dude is not here, why don't you let me, you know—escort you?"

"Mike." I was totally flustered. "That's dumb. You should ask someone who could be a real date. Half the girls in the junior class would kill to go with you."

"I doubt that," he said, looking embarrassed.

"Okay, three quarters." That made him laugh. *Shut up Morgan,* I scolded myself, *why are you flirting with him?*

Mike smiled. "The thing is, I don't want to just go through the motions with someone I'm not crazy about."

"That's how I feel too," I said. *No! Disagree with him! Be unpleasant! What are you, on automatic boy pilot?*

"See? We have something in common already." He wiped his wet hands on his jeans. "Bottom line, I'm kind of freaked out by the whole prom-date phenomenon. The junior prom was always kind of a joke, you know? But this year it's so serious, with the tuxes and the dresses and everything. . . ."

Mrs. Blainsvoort, I thought grimly. *This is all her fault.*

Mike was looking at me with those warm, chocolate-brown eyes. "The fact that you're the only girl at school who's not making a huge deal out of this just makes me feel really comfortable asking you." The melting ice water was dripping down my forearm, but I couldn't bring myself to move.

"Plus you're cool," Mike went on, "and it would be fun to dance and hang out with you and all our pals. So why don't we go together, as friends, and have a good time? No pressure. Okay?"

No pressure, right. But I could imagine it: Supercute Mike would look so handsome in a tux, and I would be feeling like pretty hot stuff myself in that knockout dress, and there would be *couples, couples, couples* everywhere, slow dancing under the soft lights and stealing kisses when the chaperones weren't looking. . . .

Wouldn't it be the absolute definition of pathetic to sit there saying, *No no no, we're just friends* all night long? Wouldn't it be far better, or at least easier, to sit home on my birthday, missing Colin and eating junk food and watching movies with Tammy, and pretend the junior prom was not happening at all?

There was no sign of ice in my hand anymore, just a cold puddle that was starting to overflow. I dashed to the sink and spread the fingers of my cupped hand, letting the water trickle down the drain.

"I'll think about it," I said.

"Great." Then he kissed me on the cheek, just casually, and left, and I thought, *No no no.*

Do not start to glimmer, Mike Fitch. Do not even go there.

But maybe it was already too late.

sixteen

thanks to the SportShoe shop and a dip into my saved allowance, I had a nice new pair of Converse high tops to trade Colin for his old Nikes.

But when to make the swap? Saturday was the day of the robot competition, and Sunday—too soon!—Colin was heading back to Ireland. Friday after school I had to bring the gnome sisters for a trial double date with Jolly Dan and the elf. I planned to deliver Colin's old sneakers to Jolly Dan then too, assuming, of course, that the date worked out and Jolly Dan held up his end of the bargain. Leprechauns were known to be tricky about stuff like that.

So today, Thursday, was not only the best but the only day to nab Colin's shoes. Mom was working as usual, and since my dad finally had a job interview, I was stuck babysitting Tammy after school.

Perfect, I thought. Tammy would be my secret, irresistible, Colin-attracting weapon.

"Here," I said to her, as I dialed his number. "Tell him you need an emergency soccer coaching for your big game tomorrow."

Tammy had all her second-grade homework worksheets scattered on the couch around her, to conceal the fact that her eyes were glued to the television. "I don't *feel* like playing soccer," she said, staring at the cartoon. "I feel like watching *SpongeBob.*"

I stood directly in front of the TV, blocking her view. "Get him over here. Cry if you have to," I said, handing her the phone. "You can do it, Tam. You know how to whine and beg and get what you want better than anyone I know."

"Wow, thank you, Morgan!" Tammy was so pleased by the compliment she didn't even protest about missing her show. "You're good at stuff too!"

She put the phone to her ear and waited for him to answer. "Hello, Colin!" she said, in her most adorable little girl voice. "This is your friend Tammy Rawlinson speaking. . . ."

Colin showed up an hour later, frazzled and pale, but putty in the hands of a cute, manipulative kid. Just as I'd hoped, he kicked off his Nikes and put on his soccer cleats before heading out into the yard. Reluctantly Tammy changed into her soccer clothes too and went outside, where she promptly starting chasing imaginary fireflies.

I could tell this soccer practice was not going to last long, so I didn't waste any time. As soon as Colin was distracted I made the switch, putting out the new Cons I'd bought and hiding his Nikes in the back of my closet. *Note to self*, I thought. *Buy Febreze and spray closet liberally*.

"What's up with Baby Beckham?" Colin wheezed, after ten minutes of trying to get Tammy to play. "I thought she was keen to learn how to blast through the goalkeeper's defenses."

"She is," I assured him. "She'll focus in a minute. She's been in school all day; she needs to unwind."

He shrugged and turned back to Tammy, now digging for worms in a garden bed. "Rawlinson," he said sternly, the soccer ball tucked under his arm, "this is yer coach speakin'. I've got to get back to HQ, there's a half-painted thingamabub in the lab, waiting for its final conversion into the bionic supergnome that'll win fame and fortune for yours truly. So let's play some football and call it a night, eh?"

"Not now," Tammy said, poking around in the mud with a stick. "I almost got a worm."

Colin dropped the ball on the ground. "What about the big game tomorrow?"

"Oh, you know," Tammy said dreamily. She dropped the stick and started to skip in circles on the grass. "It's just a game."

Meanwhile, I occupied myself by looking in on the gnomes. The card-playing gnomes were still playing, and the ale-swilling gnomes were still swilling, though I could swear the mugs were only half as full as the last time I'd checked.

Then I took a peek at Tux and Taffy, beneath the raspberry bush. Taffy was facing the shrub, with her back turned toward Tux.

"Try to be friendly, now," I said, turning her around. She

didn't answer, which was a good thing because just then Colin came running up to me. He looked very unhappy.

"Where are me trainers?" He held the new high tops in one hand.

"Surprise!" I said weakly. "I got you new ones."

"But I don't want new trainers." I'd hardly ever seen Colin get angry before. "I want me old Nikes."

"In this country we call them sneakers," I tried to joke. "And you needed new ones. They were all worn out."

"Morgan," he said slowly. "The motherly gesture is much appreciated, but those are me lucky trainers, and between now and Sunday I need all the luck I can get. If I win this competition it'll partly make up for all the—well, whatever it is that's going on with me. So if I could just have me old shoes back? Please?"

"Oh, no!" I lied, feeling sick. "I threw them out already."

As if to assist me in my fib, a Town of East Norwich sanitation truck drove down the street, hungrily munching its contents into pulp.

Colin looked ready to punch something, or cry, but instead he walked over to where Tammy had left the soccer ball and gave it a furious kick. It sailed into the neighbor's yard.

"Sorry," he muttered. "I'm so tired I can't think straight. I'd better get back to school, then." He wiped his forehead with the hem of his T-shirt. "Luck being no substitute for effort, as me grandpap would say."

"I'm sorry," I blurted. "Sorry about Tammy. Sorry about the shoes."

"Forget it." He sounded so weary. "That bit about the math project, that was all bollocks, then?"

"Half bollocks. I did have math homework. I'm sorry about that too." Now I was the one who was ready to cry. "I wanted to surprise you."

"I'm sick of surprises, and that's the bloody truth." He took a small square envelope out of his pocket and held it out to me. "Here's the latest, by the way. I'm not opening them anymore."

I took the envelope. "Don't you want to know what it says?"

"At the moment, all I want is an explanation. And me lucky trainers back. And a good night's sleep." Colin looked away. "And to go home, frankly."

By home, of course, he meant Ireland, a wide ocean away from me, my crazy family, my unwelcome gifts and my annoying half-truths.

I shoved the envelope in my pocket, too upset to even care what it said. *Just wait,* I wanted to call after him as he strode off in the direction of the bus stop. *Those old sneakers are about to bring you the best luck you've ever had.* But he was already gone.

the first official warning from the lawn police arrived that evening.

"Look at this," my mom said, the letter from the block association clutched in her hand. "It says if you don't get rid of those *things* we are going to be fined, and that's the last thing we need right now."

"The interview went well." It was after dinner. Dad had removed his tie but he was still wearing his dress shirt and suit trousers. I guess he was so glad to have an excuse to put on work clothes he didn't want to take them off. "Stop worrying about money! I'll have a new job before you know it."

"*That* has nothing to do with *this*, Daniel," Mom said, waving the letter around. "This is about you and your weird collection of eyesores—"

"You are overstressed," my dad announced, "because you're working too much. That's why you're overreacting."

"I'm working too much?" Mom's face went nearly white. "You've been out of work for four months—"

"It's not four—"

"*Exactly* four months," she went on, "and then you dare criticize me for working too much? Are you jealous? Is that what this is about? Are you trying to sabotage the business that I've built up so diligently, which by the way is the only thing paying our bills at the moment?"

"Sabotage?" my dad exclaimed. "Where the hell—excuse me—where the heck is that coming from?"

"I'm a professional declutterer!" Mom wailed in a way that was positively Tammy-like. "I get rid of people's junk and organize what's left! What does it do to my credibility to have these horrible, horrible *tchotchkes* all over my own lawn?"

"What's 'tchotchkes'?" asked Tammy, in a frightened voice. "Is it a bad word?"

"Yes! Yes!" Mom sputtered. "It's the worst word in the universe! It's what your daddy loves better than me!"

Then Mom started to cry.

Not. Good.

* * *

It took me a long time to convince Tammy that Dad wasn't having an affair with a Miss Tchotchkes, though the idea of such a person—I imagined a busty secretary whose desk was buried in Precious Moments figurines and plastic souvenir snow globes—would have been pretty funny on a happier day. My parents, without even asking if I would babysit for the evening after I'd already watched Tammy all afternoon, had grabbed their coats, climbed into Dad's car and driven off. Whether it was to an all-night lawyer's office to file for divorce or a roadside motel to kiss and make up, I had no idea.

For once, Tammy didn't freak out under stress—I guess she figured Mom and Dad had that covered—so I spent the rest of the evening listening to her jabber about the stunt Marcus pulled during independent reading while the teacher wasn't looking (it involved boogers, naturally) and some silly Saint Patrick's Day project her class would be doing over the weekend.

"I tried to tell Miss Wallace that leprechauns are controversial," Tammy said, as I tucked her in bed. "But she doesn't listen to me."

"She'll figure it out someday. Sweet dreams, brat." Tammy stuck out her tongue at me and waggled it, just like Gene Simmons from Kiss, and promptly rolled over to sleep.

With Tammy in bed and my parents in parts unknown, I finally worked up the nerve to open the envelope Colin had given me. My hands were shaking as I tore the flap—not because I was worried about what was inside; I knew it was probably just more faery mischief—but at the memory of how truly pissed off at me Colin had been. I wondered if things could ever be the way they used to be between us. At the moment, I doubted it.

Still, I thought, *I have to do what it takes to save him. Even if it means he never speaks to me again.*

Inside the envelope was a printed invitation, which I quickly scanned. The first words I saw were "East Norwich Country Club."

It felt like my heart was trying to twist itself into a pretzel. Had I been a complete idiot? Had Colin planned to ask me to the junior prom all along? Had he changed his return ticket to Ireland, just to surprise me? And then I'd stupidly blown it by stealing his shoes and not telling him the truth about what was really going on, until now he hated me forever?

I calmed myself down and looked more closely at the invitation. I knew that the real junior prom tickets were black ink on thin cardboard, in keeping with Mrs. Blainsvoort's tight-fisted budget. But this was a foil-stamped invitation in gold ink on heavy green card stock, and the edges were trimmed with matching velvet ribbon. It read:

YOU ARE CORDIALLY INVITED TO

The Spring Faery Ball

Incredibly festive attire, please!

Thursday, March 20th,
Beginning at seven o'clock
and ending maybe never!

at

the East Norwich Country Club
On that big road with all the cars
(enter by the lobby fountain)

Thursday night at the East Norwich Country Club? That was the same time, same place as the East Norwich High School junior prom.

Good thing I bought a dress, I thought. *Because if everything works out with Jolly Dan, I'll be dancing with Colin on prom night after all.*

seventeen

When i woke up friday morning, the gnomes were gone.

I discovered this when I stepped outside to do a weather check before making my final outfit decision for the day. Kind of like the groundhog, I guess.

I stood on the front steps, barefoot in pajamas, and there they were—or weren't. No gnomes. Just a nice, well-groomed, tchotchke-free suburban lawn. Something the neighbors could be proud of. You could practically feel the property values rising.

Or maybe that was terror I felt rising, crawling up my spine like a million ants in search of a picnic.

I ran all over the yard, looking behind shrubs and under bushes. No gnomes.

"Glendryn? Drenwyn?" Nothing.

I checked the garage, my bare feet leaving wet prints on the concrete floor. There were no fekkin' gnomes, anywhere.

No wonder I hadn't heard any yelling when my parents got up this morning. Maybe I should have been glad that my dad had caved in and my parents' marriage was saved, but those two gnome girls had a double date with destiny, and if they didn't show up my whole plan was ruined. All I could think of was the rats . . . *rats forced to endure prolonged sleep deprivation exhibited disoriented behavior, weight loss and eventually death.* . . .

Despite my hysteria, Dad refused to answer a single question until he and I were alone in the car, on the way to school. Even then he was evasive.

"The one-mile rule," he muttered. "Wait until we're a mile from the house."

"Dad, please," I begged. "I just want to know where they are. You didn't"—I could barely say it—"you didn't bring them to the dump, did you?"

My dad's eyes darted around like the lying weasel he apparently was. He watched the odometer, and I held my breath. "That's what I told your mother," he said, as the mile clicked over. "But I didn't. I couldn't."

"Oh thank God!" I let myself start breathing again. "Where are they?"

He drove another half-mile before he spoke. "Fine," he said, through a clenched jaw. "But you have to swear you won't tell your mother, Morgan! I'm *so* serious. If you rat me out I will *not* pay for your college education, not one penny. Got it?"

"Got it."

"Or your wedding."

Like I could ever get married. If I couldn't deliver those gnome girls to their date with Jolly Dan, I'd have to join a convent or something.

"I swear, Dad! Just tell me!"

"You know the ministorage place, near the train station?"

"Yes."

"They open at five a.m." His voice was a grim monotone, like a character in a spy movie. "I brought the gnomes there this morning. I begged the guy to let me pay cash for the room so your mother wouldn't see it on the AmEx bill."

Colin's old sneakers were in a shoebox wrapped in a plastic, stink-proof bag inside my backpack. I knew what I had to do.

"Dad, I need the key."

"What key?"

"To the ministorage. Please. I just need it today and then I'll give it back."

"Why do you need the key?"

"I can't tell you," I said, with the conviction that comes from speaking the pure truth in a moment of total desperation. "Because it's a secret, the kind of secret I can never tell, and I never will—"

"Morgan, *what* are you talking about—"

"—just the same way I will *never* break the promise I just made to you about not telling Mom that you lied to her about trashing the gnomes. Never. I swear."

Whew. Dad and I were deeply into mutual-blackmail territory now. But we seemed to understand each other.

"It's room one-one-one-four." He reached into his shirt

pocket and tossed me the key. "We won't speak of this again." And then he stared straight ahead and drove me to school like nothing had happened.

My locker door wouldn't close after I crammed in the shoebox with Colin's Nikes, so I stood there trying to re-arrange all my textbooks and gym clothes before the home-room bell rang. Sarah's locker was two down from mine, and she watched me struggle. "I heard you got an invitation," she said.

My heart skipped a beat—*how does she know about the Spring Faery Ball?*—but then I realized she was talking about Mike.

"Yeah," I said casually. "I didn't give him an answer yet, though."

"Leaning yes or leaning no?"

Leaning yes, I was about to say. Now that I knew I had to go to prom, there was really no way to avoid the Mike situa-tion. But before I could answer, Sarah held up a hand.

"On second thought, don't tell me. Tell Mike first, and then tell me. But you can't tell him right now. He's home sick."

"Sick?" I repeated, dumbly. "What's wrong with him?"

"Dunno, sounds like he's coming down with the flu or something. He called Dylan this morning and said he could barely get out of bed, he was just feeling super tired."

"Oh no!" I sounded more tragic than I meant to. "That's terrible!"

"Why? You two didn't make out, did you?" Sarah smiled mischievously. "Are you worried you might have caught something from him?"

"No," I said, knowing that the truth was exactly the opposite. "I'm just sorry he's sick." I shoved the locker door with my shoulder and it shut, barely.

"He'll be fine by prom, I'm sure. He told Dylan that even his feet hurt. Funny, huh?"

Oh, yeah. The bell rang, and I thought of the rats again. *Hilarious.*

the bus didn't stop at the ministorage place, but it let me off close enough to walk, and I found room 1114 without any trouble. Dad must have been really flustered when he'd loaded all the gnomes in before dawn. They were heaped in piles and jammed in every which way.

"Hey," I whispered. "Drenwyn? Glendryn? Are you in there?"

"Mmmmmmph!" I heard from near the top of the pile. And then an answering "Mmmmmph!" from down below.

"Pardon me," I said, as I rummaged through the gnomes.

"Sure." I heard a crabby voice from the bottom of the pile. "Take *them* out! Take out the *sisters!* Leave the rest of us here to *suffocate!*"

"Taffy Smoothcheek, if you don't shut up, we will implore the half-goddess to remove you permanently from our company. And *then* see how you like being all alone!" That was from a pair of matching bearded gnomes who, despite their silly pointy hats, apple-cheeked expressions and the comical ability to speak in perfect unison, seemed pretty ticked off.

I ignored the squabbling and looked for the girls. Finally I spotted Glendryn's crumpled pink party dress, all the way in the back.

"Ouch!" she squealed, as I grabbed her by the leg and pulled her out of the pile. "Don't forget my sister; she's in here too!"

"'Don't forget my sister! Don't forget my sister!'" Taffy mocked.

I found Drenwyn a moment later. Her berry basket was lost. She was trying not to cry about it, but she looked pretty shaken up.

"It's all right," Glendryn said soothingly. "We'll get you a new basket. We'll get *matching* baskets! How about that?"

"Sorry about the ministorage thing, guys," I said. "I don't have time to explain right now. I hope it's only temporary."

"I hope, she says!" Taffy whimpered. "What, do you mean you intend for us to live in this prison cell *forever*? What kind of goddess are you?"

"A half-goddess," I corrected impatiently, "who has to get to the mall." I shoved the sisters in my backpack and relocked the door to the storage room. That Taffy was starting to get on my nerves.

My plastic cargo and I were riding the escalators to the second floor of the mall when I got a text message:

> ddnt hve tme to cln shop
> mt me & elf @ mnglf 5
> jly dn the lprchn

Most of it was clear, but what did mnglf mean? Mango loofah? Mongolian food? And did 5 mean five o'clock? If so, what was I supposed to do for an hour with the two gnomes in my backpack? Not only was it dark and crowded and hot in there, but Colin's sneakers were jammed in the bottom, which had to be creating a noticeable funk factor. I opened the zipper a couple of inches, just for circulation.

I stopped in front of the mall directory to skim the list of store names. There was a Gap, an Old Navy, an Abercrombie & Fitch, a multiplex cinema, a Macy's, a Saks, a Barnes & Noble, a Borders, a Japanese import shop that Sarah and I always called the Hello Kitty store though they had way more stuff than that, a Hot Topic and some other faux-punk boutiques that carried edgy logo tees and stuff to streak your hair blue, Strohman's Designer Discounts, a CVS, a Body Shop, a Circuit City, an Office Max . . .

I felt some squirming in my backpack and shifted my weight until the girls settled down. Then, just as I was about to go order a Starbucks mocha latte in defeat, I saw what I was looking for, all the way at the top of the directory map, by itself, with a shiny sticker next to it that read GRAND OPENING.

Level five. Minigolf.

I had to laugh. Minigolf? Was that the perfect setting for

a first date between a leprechaun and a garden gnome, or what?

forget cutesy landscapes of windmills and ginger-bread houses. This was Lunar Minigolf, an outer-space themed, black-light funhouse that you played in the pitch dark, with Pink Floyd music piped in from invisible speakers. There were a lot of kids my age going in there, and I kept my head down in case I ran into someone from school.

I paid to play a single game of eighteen holes, grabbed a putter and went in. I didn't dare put the backpack down because the place was so dark I was afraid I'd never find it again.

"Mmph! Dark in here," I heard at one point from inside the bag.

"It's dark out here too," I muttered, taking a swing and almost landing the ball in the Lake of Perseverance.

"Try the Sea of Tranquility, it's a lot easier." I knew that mocking voice. What a perfectly gross place to run into my perfectly gross ex-boyfriend.

"Golfing alone?" Raph's white T-shirt glowed in the black light, but his face came in and out of view. "Why don't you join us?"

"No, thanks," I said. "I'm just working on my swing."

"Is that him?" my backpack squealed.

"No!" I answered sharply.

"Okay, I heard you the first time!" Raph backed off. "Yikes. You don't have to be a bitch about it."

For a second I felt bad for being rude, but then I heard Raph's voice receding as he walked across the moonscape with his friends: "Nah, she's on the rag or something. . . . Hasn't changed, same old Morgan, doesn't know how to have fun . . ."

I wondered what the odds were of me whacking a golf ball in the pitch dark with enough speed and accuracy to clock Raphael firmly on the back of his arrogant head, but I forgot all about that when I saw the next hole.

It was marked Hole 19, which would tend to indicate something unusual, right? And all the other holes had these poetic moonscape names, like the Sea of Dreams and the Ocean of Storms.

This one was called the Tunnel of Love.

"Freshen your lip gloss, girls," I said to my backpack. "I think we've arrived at your date."

Inside hole 19 was a whole other world.

We were still on the moon, but it was a different sort of moon. It was bathed in a cool, bluish—you'd have to call it moonlight, I guess. This was a moon made of green cheese, with an animatronic cow jumping over it. Beneath our feet, the ground was smiling.

"Man in the Moon, I presume?" I asked, looking down. He nodded, which made the whole place rock gently.

"Whee!" cried Glendryn and Drenwyn, so glad to be out of the backpack and scampering about. The gravitational field was accurately moonlike, and the sisters held hands and bounded and leaped through the air like they were on a trampoline.

"Ahem!"

I turned and stifled a cry of alarm.

"It's me," Jolly Dan said sheepishly. "It's Jolly Dan." He shrugged. "I thought perhaps you might not recognize me because of all the . . . improvements."

Jolly Dan's appearance had definitely changed, but whether you'd consider the changes "improvements" would depend on whether or not you had any taste. What I saw was a two-foot tall leprechaun with a George Hamilton tan, blindingly white teeth, gel-spiked hair and a beard that was braided and ribboned like the tail of a show pony. He was wearing a pair of skinny trousers, a vintage suit jacket over a loose collared shirt and black square-rimmed glasses. It was like, pint-sized cruise ship lothario meets indie rock hipster, and it was making my head hurt.

"This is my friend," Jolly Dan said, indicating a very tall, very gorgeous, very Orlando Bloomish–looking guy dressed in simple white robes. Then he said something that sounded like "Q'nessir mith'ela rahdili taurgoth," except played backward.

I stared at the tall gorgeous guy. We are talking serious, serious eye candy here.

"You will not be able to pronounce my true Elven name," the elf said. "But you can call me Elvis."

I shook off his hypnotic stare, called the gnome sisters over, and introduced them to Jolly Dan and Elvis, amidst many giggles and "isn't the moon great?" pleasantries. I guess I shouldn't have been surprised when the sisters asked me to leave.

"We may be little to you, but we're not children," Drenwyn pointed out. "We don't require a chaperone."

"After all, we have each other," Glendryn added.

So I left, but I told them I would swing by in an hour to pick them up.

"Best to keep the first date short," I said. "No offense."

"Later, crater!" called Elvis, as I half-walked, half-bounced away. Behind me, Glendryn and Drenwyn were laughing a little too hard at the elf's green-cheesy pun.

eighteen

the double date was out of my hands, so i wandered the mall, with Colin's shoes still fermenting in my backpack. I stopped at Starbucks and got my latte and then browsed through some CDs at the Virgin Megastore. For laughs, I bought myself a "Best of Kiss" collection.

I checked my phone frequently, *to keep track of the time,* I told myself, but that was bogus because I was wearing a watch. Really it was to see if Colin had called to say hi, or make a joke, or give some indication that he might still be speaking to me.

But there was nothing: no calls, no messages, no texts. I almost called him just to make sure he was okay, but I was planning to go to UConn the next day to see how his project did in the robot competition, and if I talked to him now, while he was probably still furious at me, he might tell me not to come. Overall it was better if we didn't speak.

Luckily malls suck up time as easily as they suck up money, and the hour passed quickly. Back on level five I flashed the Lunar Minigolf inkstamp on my hand, reentered and found my way to Hole 19.

The moon was deserted. The man in the moon had closed his eyes. Even the cow was gone. I bounded and bounced around for quite a while before I found him.

Yes, *him*. Jolly Dan was alone, lying facedown in the Sea of Despondency.

"Hey," I said. "Where is everybody?"

"They left." He didn't move.

"Left?" I tried not to jump to any horrible conclusions. "Where did they go?"

"How am I supposed to know?" Jolly Dan rolled onto his back and started yelling. "Ask Elvis! Your plastic friends couldn't tear their eyes off his freakishly elongated figure, and before you can say 'Kiss off, Jolly Dan,' the three of them ditched me! End. Of. Story."

Ouch. I'd heard bad date stories before, but being left stranded on the moon kind of topped them all. "Did you guys get a chance to talk about the Faery Ball?" I asked, as delicately as I could.

"Morganne, apparently you are only a half-listening sort of half-goddess," Jolly Dan roared. "Yes, those cheaply manufactured bookends talked about the Faery Ball! They are absolutely determined to go to the Faery Ball! *With Elvis.*" He sniffed. "They were just using me to get to the elf."

"That's awful," I said, while thinking, *I may have seriously underestimated those two.*

"They prefer to 'stick together,' they told me." Jolly Dan

flipped over again in the crater and kicked and pounded his fists on the lunar landscape, raising sad, silvery clouds of moondust everywhere. "I thought minigolf would make me seem taller," he moaned. "But it just made Elvis look like a giant."

I started coughing because of the dust, and my eyes watered. I reached inside my backpack looking for tissues, but all I found were Colin's sneakers. At the sight—or should I say, aroma—of the shoes, Jolly Dan got even more upset. Slowly he climbed to his feet.

"I told you, I'm not making any magic shoes for your friend unless you find me a date." His fancy new clothes were covered with dust, and there was a little leprechaun-shaped crater where he'd been laying. "And you didn't. In fact, you messed up big time!"

"I'm sorry." I didn't know what else to say. "Meeting the right person isn't easy. Sometimes it doesn't work out, but that doesn't mean you stop looking—"

"Go!" he roared. "And take that smelly footwear with you!"

the leprechaun's right. this was all my fault, i thought, on the long, pathetic bus ride home from the mall.

If I were honest, I had to admit that I'd known the gnome girls were not quite right for Jolly Dan. They were the perfect size on the outside, sure, but not a good match on the inside. And the double-dating with twins idea was way too much to handle for a guy's first attempt at a coed outing.

I'd been so eager to get Colin's magic shoes that I pushed for something to happen that I knew in my heart was doomed to fail. Now, because of mĕ, Jolly Dan had been through the worst date of his life, and not just because it was the only date of this life. The Spring Faery Ball was only days away, and Colin was no closer to getting unenchanted than he was before.

Maybe I'd left my magic mojo behind in Ireland after all.

Or, I thought, *maybe the goddess part of me was the part that had known the gnome sisters were a bad idea, and I'd been too self-ish and stubborn to listen.*

When I got home, Tammy was ransacking the house look-ing for any empty shoebox for a school project, so I gave her the one Colin's shoes had been in. Then I stashed his now very unlucky trainers in a plastic Lucky Lou's bag, to contain the biohazard fumes.

I stowed the bag under my bed. *Colin's life might be ruined by a faery enchantment that I was too much of a loser to undo,* I thought miserably, *but at least he'd gotten a new pair of Cons out of it.*

And Tammy got a shoebox. From the way she jumped around with joy, you'd think I'd given her a diamond tiara.

On Saturday, my parents' fragile peace treaty was trashed like origami in a paper shredder when we were fined five hundred bucks by the Lawn Police. The notice was left in the mailbox quite early in the morning, in a nasty-looking en-velope with the word *Violation* written on it in fat red marker.

Five hundred dollars? Great, I thought, amidst all the yelling. *Now I'll* never *learn to drive.*

And why would we get fined now? Now, after my dad had finally packed up all his precious gnomes and hauled them away, even if he'd been less than perfectly honest with my mom about their ultimate destination?

Because Glendryn and Drenwyn were joyously pirouetting dead center on the front lawn, that's why. Maybe Elvis had given them a lift home—whatever had happened, the threesome date had definitely left a fresh coat of twinkle on their eyes. I was glad to see they were all right, but their display of morning-after euphoria had several not-so-euphoric consequences:

Consequence number one: the five hundred dollar fine. I figured Dad could just take it out of the money he would now *not* be spending on my college tuition.

Consequence number two: Mom stopped speaking to Dad. He swore up and down that he hadn't put the gnomes there, but in Mom's pissed-off universe, gnomes on the lawn were my dad's doing. End. Of. Story. As Jolly Dan would say.

Consequence number three: Not surprisingly, Dad was *way* angry at me. I'd known where the gnomes were, I'd briefly had possession of the key—I was guilty until proven innocent in his eyes. The only good thing was that he couldn't tell my mom about his suspicions, because then his whole deceitful scheme about putting the gnomes in mini-storage would come to blinding, marriage-ending light.

"Betrayed! By my own daughter! On the Ides of March!" he hissed, as he drove me to UConn for the robotics contest. I didn't know what he was talking about, but you didn't need to be a rocket scientist to understand that I was in big trouble, even if the exact terms of my punishment wouldn't be revealed until a later date.

I hope Colin and Alice win, I thought wearily, as Dad's furious rant droned on and on. *It would be such a relief if at least one not-sucky thing happened today.*

they lost.

Correction: They came in last. Dead last, out of twelve teams. Colin had been telling the truth about lacking talent in the arts-and-crafts department. The papier mâché body he'd built using the gnome mould looked kind of dented and mutant, like a zombie toddler from an especially sick horror film. Whatever advantage he'd hoped to gain from the "anthropomorphic" presentation of their robot was instantly wiped out by the WTF expression on people's faces when they saw it.

As for technical performance, luck was not on their side, or maybe Colin's mental fog had messed up his work on the programming more than he and Alice had realized. Their task was to build a robot that could maneuver around obstacles, retrieve small objects and place them in a slowly moving container with ninety percent accuracy or better. To my horror, Colin had named the robot Nike, after the "lucky trainers" he thought I'd destroyed.

Nike did fine in the precompetition demonstration, but when the judges were watching the robot seemed to get stage fright. There were power supply failures, frozen hard drives and software malfunctions. Alice looked ready to kill, and the judges scowled and wrote copious notes on their clipboards.

After they'd gone, we sat and watched Nike score shot after shot, dropping its cargo in the basket every time. By then, of course, it was too late. At one point I even overheard Alice fast-talking one of the judges, explaining how Nike's physical design hadn't been her idea and asking to have her work evaluated separately.

"That's teamwork for ye. If I wasn't so tired I'd go give her a piece of me mind," Colin said, yawning. "But I just want the day to be over so's I can lie down."

Is this what his life will be like from now on? I thought glumly. *Failure and exhaustion? All because I couldn't find a date for a leprechaun?*

later, back in his dorm room, i offered to help him pack.

"Not much to do, really," he said, collapsing on his bare cot. "Thanks for comin' today, though, Mor. Sorry we made such a poor showing."

"Does it matter a lot that you didn't win?" I was rolling sock balls from the laundry basket just to keep my hands busy, and he watched me in silence for minute before answering.

"I'm on partial scholarship at DCU, ye know. And they review the funding every term. I was hoping a win here would guarantee me a free ride for next year." He looked out the window for a minute, then back at me. "Me grades have been suffering because of all the poor sleeping and whatnot, so I'll just have to hope for the best."

"Alice seemed pretty upset." Not that I cared about Alice's feelings—but maybe Colin did?

"No doubt she is, but her armor's tough enough to take the hit." He smiled a little. "I may have done less than me best this time around, but at least I know me stuff. Alice doesn't have a third of the technical know-how she pretends to. You can't get through life just bossing people around and making excuses. Maybe now that she's had a taste of humiliation she'll crack open a book or two. And," he added, "she doesn't have any worries about scholarship money; her da owns some big factory in China, mass-producing plastic thingamabubs. She's loaded."

Mass produced plastic thingamabubs from China . . . someone has to make them, I guess. I kept folding Colin's clothes, trying to fill each T-shirt and pair of chinos with all the stuff I felt but couldn't say.

"So," Colin said as he watched me, "tell me about this prom business. Who's the lucky fella?"

I folded a shirt. I thought of Mike. I didn't say anything.

"Don't try and pull one over on yer ol' pal Colin," he prodded. "Somebody's asked ye, right?"

I made a sockball out of two mismatched socks and tossed it in his duffel bag. "Yes," I said. "Somebody's asked me."

With effort, Colin swung his legs over the side of the cot and sat up. "Is he a nice bloke? A good egg?"

"He's very nice." I was careful to avoid eye contact.

"Well, ye said yes, didn't ye?"

At that point I guess I must have started to looked tragic or something, because Colin came over and took my hand.

"Hey, Mor," he said softly. "You're not waiting around for me, are ye?"

"Don't you want me to?" I looked up and caught his gaze,

and this time I didn't look away. There it was, the question I'd been wanting to ask him, for months and months—since the day I left Ireland, in fact.

Why had I waited so long to ask? Because I knew what the answer would be. And yet—a person could hope, couldn't she?

He exhaled heavily, but didn't let go of my hand. "It's times like this I miss smokin' somethin' fierce. Now, lass. That's an unfair question and ye know it."

"Why is it unfair?" I sounded as stubborn as Tammy.

"Because if I say yes it'll only encourage ye, and that wouldn't be right"—he stopped me from interrupting with a look—"no, it wouldn't, Mor, because I can't be here for ye." He paused. "And if I say no, that's not the whole bloody truth, is it?"

I looked down at the ground, my heart leaping and breaking at the same time.

"Stop staring at yer trainers," he said, trying to make me smile. "What are ye thinkin', then?"

"That I could really go for a kiss right now." I looked up at him and his face was *thisclose* to mine, and he looked so gorgeous and irresistible and thoroughly Colin-like, I could hardly stand it. Neither one of us looked away, but neither one of us moved either.

"A kiss, eh? That'd be sweet, for sure." He squeezed my hand. "Say yes to the good egg, Mor. Yer still in high school. Have some fun."

"Okay," I said, in a voice that came from someplace far, far away.

"And, no hanky panky now. Yer only sixteen."

"Not for long. My birthday's this week."

"Is it?" He smiled. "I'm glad to hear it. It's about time you grew up some."

"Shut up," I said, trying not to cry.

"Hey," he said, in a softer voice. "Send me a picture of you in the fancy dress, would ye? I'd give anything to see it."

That did it. It took every molecule of strength I had not to dissolve into huge, miserable sobs. Unfortunately I was one molecule short.

"Promise?" he asked again, and held me as I cried.

I promise was stuck in my throat, but that was way more than I was able to say at the moment, so I just gulped and nodded and blubbered. Colin handed me a sock to blow my nose in.

"Don't worry, it's clean," he deadpanned.

"Not anymore," I said, as I blew.

Then we both laughed, and I knew everything was fine between us again. But it was time for both of us to go home.

nineteen

All I could do Sunday, all day long, was watch the clock and imagine Colin on his journey, each step taking him farther and farther away from me.

I pictured him riding the bus to the airport, checking his luggage, waiting on line at the security checkpoint and dozing in the waiting area by the gate. Then, as the time for his flight approached, he'd board the plane, toss his carry-on luggage in the overhead compartment, settle into his seat and fasten his seat belt. He'd probably say something funny to the people next to him. Lucky them, whoever they were.

When it was the exact time of his flight I imagined him leaning back in his seat as the plane took off. The Aer Lingus jet would gain altitude before swerving and banking over the edge of North America and heading out to sea. It would fly a long, high arc across the ocean, soaring above the clouds for hours until it touched down on the other side, on the impossibly green grass of Ireland.

By the time I went to bed, Colin would be home. Just in time to spend Saint Patrick's Day with his grandfather, as he'd promised.

Tracking Colin's location in my head reminded me of something Mom liked to do with Tammy at Christmas. Together they'd visit this website that allegedly showed Santa's real-time location on Christmas Eve, tracking his flight path all night long as he delivered toys around the globe in his supersonic sleigh. "NORAD Tracks Santa," it was called.

The site's high-tech language always cracked me up: Their *infrared sensors could detect the heat signature of Rudolph's nose, using a powerful military radar system and multiple satellites in geosynchronous orbit, tens of thousands of miles above the earth.* "These are the same satellites NORAD uses to detect incoming missiles!" it cheerfully proclaimed. Personally I never found the idea of incoming missiles to be particularly Christmasy.

NORAD tracks Colin. That's what I wanted: a little radar blip showing me Colin's location, mile by mile, on land and sea and air, as he headed far, far away from me once more. I had no idea when we'd see each other again, or if I'd ever be able to break the enchantment that threatened to ruin his life.

And the whole time he'd been in Connecticut, we'd never even kissed.

*   *   *

With me moping around and the parents back in
fight mode, poor Tammy was left struggling to put together
her Saint Patrick's Day project by herself.

At various points during the day I saw her fussing with
the shoebox, but I was too depressed to pay much attention.
Paints came out. Bits of tape and torn pieces of tissue paper
were everywhere. It was after dinner before she finally approached me for help.

"I am almost done," she said bravely, although she was
clearly on her last nerve. "All I need are some pennies. And a
mug."

Under one arm Tammy was holding the shoebox, which
was now painted green, with green tissue paper taped over
the top. In the other hand she was holding a can of root beer.

"What is that?" I asked, clueless.

"It's a leprechaun trap. We're supposed to catch one and
bring it in to class tomorrow, for Saint Patrick's Day." She
looked up at me, and there was green paint smudged all over
her face. "I kept telling my teacher they're controversial and
we might not get any, but she didn't listen."

Great, I thought miserably. *First my dad imprisons the
gnomes in a tiny cell, and now my sister is setting traps for leprechauns.* Forget about the Lawn Police—if there was an AS-
PCA for mistreatment of pint-sized magical beings, they
were going to be pulling up in their squad cars any minute
now to drag us all to headquarters.

"The pennies are bait," Tammy went on. "The root beer
too, but I need to put it in a mug because this can is too big
for a leprechaun to open. They're very small, you know." She
looked at me with big wise eyes. "I have to hide the trap in

the garden. Will you help me?" Her voice quavered. "It's kind of dark outside."

I took some pennies from my wallet and found a minia-ture souvenir beer stein my parents had gotten at a wedding. "Here," I said, showing it to her. "This is the right size for a leprechaun, don't you think?"

Together we hid the box under the bushes outside and laid a trail of pennies to the entrance. With great concentra-tion, Tammy filled the tiny mug with root beer.

"Perfect," she said when we were done. "I will catch the best leprechaun of anyone in my class." Then she went inside to watch TV.

I couldn't imagine Jolly Dan being tricked by a painted shoebox. But then I had a crazy idea, and the more I thought about it, the more I thought, *Why not?* Jolly Dan still didn't have a date to the Faery Ball, and I desperately needed an-other chance to get that enchantment off poor Colin, and—it couldn't hurt to try, anyway.

So, later that night, after Tammy was asleep, I snuck out and added some bait of my own to the trap.

I put some pink nail polish inside, and a picture of Or-lando Bloom I downloaded off the Internet. Then I added my favorite pink lip gloss, just for luck.

This was not just a leprechaun trap anymore.

This was a *girl* leprechaun trap.

feeling kind of stupid, i set my alarm for five a.m. to make sure I got to the trap before Tammy woke up. I fig-ured the odds of there being anyone in there were a zillion to one, but what if I was wrong? I sure didn't want Tammy dragging some poor leprechaun into Miss Wallace's class for show and tell.

As for my own girl-bait additions to the trap—granted, they probably made the odds ten zillion to one. But there was still that one, and that was enough to explain why, Monday morning, in the predawn darkness, I was trudging along the wet grass with a flashlight, even though I was almost completely certain that, when I crouched down low next to the raspberry bush and pushed the green tissue paper aside, the leprechaun trap would be completely uninhabited.

It wasn't.

And when I saw what—I mean, who—was in the trap, a lot of things suddenly started to make perfect sense.

"Taffy Smoothcheek!" I exclaimed. "Are you—are you a leprechaun?"

"No," she cried, hurriedly wiping the lip gloss off her lips. "No no no! I'm a misfit gnome, that's all!"

I stared at her, and she stared at me. A penny dropped from her tight little fist and rolled into the grass.

"It took more than gnome magic to get out of that ministorage, Taffy," I said.

"But I'm not," she whimpered. "I'm an Occasional Exception!"

I looked at her crab-apple, not very gnomelike face. I thought about her grouchy, not very gnomelike temper. "Perhaps," I said. "But did you ever consider the *possibility* that maybe—just maybe—"

"Of course not," she said. She looked around like someone might be eavesdropping, and lowered her voice. "But I do have a confession to make. I like shoes."

"Shoes?"

"Shhhh!" She shushed me wildly. "I don't have the right tools to make them, but I draw the designs. I've done it since I was a child."

She pulled a tiny sketchbook out of her apron pocket and showed me the pages. Shoes, shoes and more shoes. Some of them were pretty stylish, especially if you liked buckles.

"Doesn't that make it even more likely that you might be a—" I saw her wince, but pressed on. "You know. A lepre—"

"But if I'm a—what you said I might be," she interrupted, quickly hiding the book from sight, "that means I'm a boy, because there *are* no female—what you said I might be." Taffy started to tear up. "And I don't wanna be a boy. I don't *feel* like a boy. Boys are doofuses, most of the time!"

"Sometimes they are. But, Taffy," I said gently, "maybe everyone's wrong. Maybe there *are* female leprechauns. Maybe they're all like you—they don't believe that they exist, because everyone says they don't, so they think they're just misfit gnomes."

"Or unpopular dwarf," she said, weeping.

"Right," I agreed, "or, you know, uncool trolls, or whatever."

"I knew a troll like that once," Taffy sniffed. "She had *no* friends! It was sad!"

"Exactly," I said. "I'm just saying, maybe it's time to ignore what you've been told, and admit what you really are."

Taffy heaved a final sob, chugged the rest of the root beer and wiped her mouth on her sleeve. "Okay," she said, pulling herself together. "Maybe you're right. Maybe I am a girl leprechaun. It would explain a lot. But to be honest, I'm not sure how to tell."

On the assumption that the differences between boy and girl leprechauns were more or less the same as those between boy and girl humans, I quickly explained to Taffy how to tell.

"Saint Patrick preserve us!" she exclaimed, as she peeked beneath her apron. "I *am* a girl leprechaun!"

Then she started crying all over again.

"Don't be sad, Taffy." I offered her a tissue from my pocket. "Being the first official girl leprechaun in recorded history is kind of awesome, if you think about it."

"I know." She dabbed her eyes with the tissue. "Now I'm crying because I'm happy. Deep inside, I've always known I wasn't like all the other gnomes." Then, through her tears, she smiled what could only be described as a crinkly leprechaun smile, and winked at me like a pro. "And finally, I know why!"

To be honest, that made me feel kind of teary myself.

"Not another gnome!" Jolly Dan cried.

By the time I got home from school Monday afternoon, Taffy Smoothcheek had totally embraced her new identity. She'd spent the day hiding in the yard, making shoe-shaped mud pies (Glendryn and Drenwyn had been put back in the garage, of course). Her eagerness to meet one of her own kind was so extreme I thought she might scare Jolly Dan, so when I took her to see him I asked her to wait outside the door of his shop while I explained the situation.

"She's not another gnome, I promise you."

"Then what?" he said scornfully. "I'm not interested in a giantess like you!"

"No, she's just your size. She's just your—everything. Jolly Dan," I said, feeling incredibly nervous all of a sudden, "she's a girl leprechaun."

"No!" he bellowed. "Impossible! I don't believe you."

"Don't be so close minded," I scolded. "You keep telling me how leprechauns are solitary. If that's the case, you'd never get the chance to compare your, uh, differences with each other. How would you even know if some were female and some were male?"

At this he started to stammer and blush. "It's an understandable mistake," I went on, though I hardly thought that it was. "Haven't you ever met a leprechaun who seemed the slightest bit *different* from you?"

"Wait a minute," said Jolly Dan, the light dawning. "You don't mean—the *beardless* leprechauns?"

"They're girls, you dumdum!" I threw up my hands and almost smacked the ceiling.

"But I thought girls wore pink dresses and had long hair with ribbons? I thought they giggled and acted silly?"

"Jolly Dan! That is *not* the difference between boys and girls, okay? There's a lot more to it."

"Like what?"

Sheesh! Was it really my job to explain the facts of life to this entire species? "Like—oh for Pete's sake! Taffy, would you come in here, please?"

I opened the tiny front door, and in walked Taffy. And when Jolly Dan Dabby and Taffy Smoothcheek got their first look at each other, I didn't have to do very much more explaining. Although, to be honest, other than Jolly Dan having a beard and Taffy not, there really wasn't much physical difference between the two of them.

"Don't they have health class in leprechaun schools?" I said under my breath.

"They used to, in the old days," said Jolly Dan, gazing at Taffy like, well, like he'd never seen a girl before, "because, as I recall, there was some grown-up 'thing' they didn't want us young ones to do."

"I remember that too," said Taffy, her face brightening. "But then they decided that the best way to convince us not to do this 'thing' was to not tell us what it was. So they stopped having the classes altogether."

Jolly Dan nodded. "I guess we've gotten a bit confused as a result."

I'll say, I thought. But I had other business to finish up.

"Now, Jolly Dan," I said, laying Colin's sneakers on the workbench. "Do we have a deal?"

He looked at Taffy, and at me, and bowed his head.

"The finest pair of hand-sewn boots I have ever made shall be yours, in time for the Spring Faery Ball."

"Thank you." I knew he was showing off for Taffy, but I didn't care. "You rock."

Taffy took a long, deep sniff, and her eyes grew round. "What's that smell?" she asked.

"It's shoes," Jolly Dan explained reverently. "They smell like leather. And feet."

"What a wonderful smell," Taffy said, awestruck. "It smells like—home."

twenty

tammy was not the only kid in Miss Wallace's class who failed to bring a leprechaun to school. In fact, not a single one of her classmates managed to catch one.

"Bummer," I said, when I finally got home from the mall and she gave me the rundown. She was pretty disappointed. Part of me wished I could tell her that her trap had worked, but I knew that was a bad idea, so I poured each of us a bedtime bowl of Lucky Charms cereal, just to cheer her up.

"Maybe leprechauns are not controversial *or* missological," she said somberly, staring at the tiny, artificially-flavored marshmallow bits floating in the milk. "Maybe they're just bogus."

"Or maybe," I said, shoving a big spoonful in my mouth, "they're just really, really tricky."

I gave myself a few minutes to enjoy the sugar rush, and then I got to work. Mike Fitch was incredibly jazzed when I called and said yes, I would love to go to the junior prom with him, and he acted very sweet and *no problemo* about me being such an indecisive wimp about the whole thing. "I'm just glad you came to your senses," he joked.

And when I asked how he was feeling, he said he was completely recovered—he'd just overdosed on Red Bull and double-shot lattes and couldn't sleep for two days, but he'd cut back on the Bull and the Starbucks and now he was fine. Mysterious? Maybe, but as long as he was okay I wasn't going to question it.

I made the obligatory BFF call to Sarah right after I hung up with Mike. She was mega-psyched to hear my news, until I got to the part about how Mike and I were going purely as friends.

"Right," she scoffed. "And it's just a coincidence that Colin left for Ireland yesterday, and today you're suddenly saying yes to Mike? Two seemingly connected events, yet in reality they are completely unrelated?"

"In reality, they are," I replied. "Funny how things work out, though."

I didn't bother explaining that Colin was the one who'd made me promise to say yes to Mike in the first place. The way I looked at it, between the junior prom and the Spring Faery Ball, I'd be attending not one but two formal dances on my birthday, and I'd lined up a pretty sweet date for each of them.

Not only that, but I'd get to wear my stunning five-dollar prom dress to two different events. Talk about a bargain!

* * *

Maybe it was the total lack of clutter in her mind, but no one could put anything over on my mom for long. Tuesday morning, while I scrambled to get ready for school, head swimming with my pre-prom to-do list—*shave legs, buy clear antiperspirant, pick up magic shoes from leprechaun*—Mom decided she "wanted to talk."

"I'm glad you and Sarah are friends again," she tossed out. "I always liked her."

"Yeah, Sarah's great." My mouth was full of the home-made organic blueberry muffins my dad had baked out of sheer competitive spite. "Did you see my science notebook?"

She handed it to me, along with a napkin. "Who else are you hanging out with these days?"

Before I could take another bite of muffin it became clear that, mentally at least, Mom was starring in her own ongoing episode of *CSI: Rawlinson Family Edition*—the one about how those two gnomes got on the lawn. Dad still refused to admit that he'd put them there (which was understandable, since he hadn't). And Mom had calmed down enough to consider alternative explanations, which quickly got her singing that old hit song that all grown-ups know, "It Must Have Been Some Kind of Teenage Prank."

But to my mom's way of thinking, it had to be teens who knew about the infamous gnome collection. Otherwise why not just key the car and toilet-paper the house?

And so, based on no forensic evidence but her own iron-trap logic, Mom had come to the same conclusion as Dad, namely: Either it's Morgan's doing, or she knows something that she's not telling us.

See what I mean? The woman was scary.

"If someone might have pulled a prank to harass you," Mom said, while carefully examining the fingerprints on the stainless steel refrigerator, "your father and I want to know about it. Have you had any contact with Raphael lately?"

Mom had always disliked Raph and his crowd. It would have been so easy, but also so wrong, to blame them for the gnomes.

"No," I said. "And I'm positive Raphael didn't have anything to do with it."

"Maybe it was someone else, then." She rearranged the organic apples in the fruit bowl and studied them as if they were a clue.

"Maybe," I said, grabbing an apple for later. "Or maybe we'll never know who did it. In the meantime, would you and Dad just get over this? No matter how it happened, it's not worth it to keep arguing over a stupid prank." I put on my most serious, *Afterschool Special*–worthy expression. "I think all the parental conflict is really freaking Tammy out."

"Parental conflict?" She seemed shocked. "We don't have any parental conflict! I mean, we don't have any *serious* parental conflict. I mean—"

The look of utter *you have got to be kidding me* on my face pretty much said it all.

"I guess you're right." The fruit bowl was all messed up now but Mom didn't seem to notice; she was too busy dabbing at her eyes with a bleach-free recycled paper napkin. "I guess it was a five hundred dollar lesson to learn."

*   *   *

Mrs. Blainsvoort had been conducting an investigation of her own, apparently. Not about the gnomes. About the band.

"After doing some legwork," she said, in a cold-sounding message she left on Sarah's voice mail, "I discovered that your boyfriend's band is actually known for playing 'heavy metal.' In bizarre costumes, no less? I appreciate the cleverness of that little performance you put on for my benefit, but under the circumstances I think we'll stick with the DJ. Nice try, though."

Sarah was pissed, but Dylan laughed it off. "Come on," he said, "so we'll party to stupid dance mixes. It's just a prom, right?"

"I know," she grumbled. "I just wanted *something* subversive to happen, that's all."

Mike, on the other hand, was working the whole prom concept with gusto. He asked me what I planned to wear and I almost freaked out—coordinated outfits, eek! I didn't want to take even the first step toward acting like a couple. But he just wanted to know what color corsage to get.

"Anything but pink," I told him.

By the time Wednesday rolled around, a lot of girls in my class were cutting out for appointments to get their hair done, but the pre-prom chore I cared most about was picking up Colin's new shoes from Jolly Dan. The Strohman's saleswoman was alarmed to see me yet again, now on the day before prom.

"Is everything okay with the dress?" she said.

"Yes, yes, it's perfect," I babbled. "I just wanted to try on some—cruise wear." I grabbed a fuschia bikini and a tropical print cover-up off the racks and headed into the now-familiar dressing room and its magical mirrored portal.

Jolly Dan did not comment on my Hawaiian outfit, but he was very excited to show me what he'd made.

"These are one of a kind," he said proudly, as he placed the shoes on his workbench for me to admire. "Or, two of a kind, to be precise." He laughed. "Sorry, it's an old shoe-maker's joke."

You got that right, I thought, staring with horror at the shoes. They were thoroughly hideous buckle-top boots, very leprechaunish, but enlarged to fit Colin's human-guy-sized feet. What might have been whimsical and cute on a small magic person was just mind-bogglingly ugly at a larger scale, and I couldn't picture Colin wearing these things unless he got a job working at a theme park. To my surprise, there was a Nike swoosh logo carefully embroidered on the side of each boot.

"Why the swoosh?" I asked.

Jolly Dan's eyebrows knitted together into a long, furry line. "The what?"

"This," I explained, tapping the emblem with my finger. "It's called a swoosh."

"It was on the shoes you gave me. I thought it was his family crest." He frowned. "Do you want me to take it off?"

"No, leave it," I said quickly. "It's very family-crest-like. He'll love it." *It's probably the only thing about these boots he will like,* I thought. But magic was magic. If the shoes end the enchantment, who cared how goofy they looked?

Jolly Dan wrapped the shoes carefully in tissue paper and put them in an enormous shoebox, big enough to trap a whole family of leprechauns. "I'm very much looking forward to escorting Miss Smoothcheek to tomorrow night's festivities. I imagine we'll see you there?" He handed me the box. "Oh! One tiny thing about the boots! If you tell him they're magic, they won't work."

"What?" I was already at the door, but this stopped me in my tracks. "You mean I have to convince him to put them on . . . just because?"

"Right. Just because. But that's why I made them so fashion forward." He smiled. "I'm sure you won't have any trouble. See you at the ball!"

Colin had sent me a two-line e-mail early in the week letting me know he'd arrived safely, with a promise to write a longer note when he got unjetlagged. I heard from him on Wednesday night.

Mor,

Apologies in advance if this doesn't make sense. I keep starting over and losing my train of thought.

I expect you'll have a busy day tomorrow, what with Prince Charming whisking you to the palace in a carriage drawn by mice and all that, so I thought it best to write tonight. Happy birthday, luv. Wish I could be there to see you age in person.

The tale of my humiliating defeat on American shores did not play so well on the home front. But St. Pat's with Grandpap was a jolly blowout of Guinness and tall tales, and that cheered me some. Funny old coot—this year he dug up a picture I'd drawn as a boyo. It's of a very pretty, long-haired lass in a fancy dress. I'd say she looked like a crayon version of you, except for the long hair, of course. Hat's off to me mum for keeping it so well. The drawing looks brand new, you can still smell the Crayola.

Have a good time tomorrow—and don't forget to send the photo you promised. I'll pair it with this picture and call 'em a set.

Colin

twenty-one

"Morgan's birthday is the infernal equinox!" Tammy announced at breakfast Thursday. "Miss Wallace told us."

"Not to mention the first day of spring," Dad remarked. My family had already sung the "happy birthday" song twice, stuck a candle in my breakfast muffin and presented me with a homemade gift certificate for unlimited free driving lessons from "Mom & Dad's Cheerful and Patient Driving Academy." Cute. Cheap, but cute.

"*And* it's the day of the junior prom," added Mom, her hands briefly resting on Dad's shoulders as she passed behind him to take her seat at the table. "How come *we* never get dressed up and go out dancing anymore?"

"Anymore?" He laughed. "Did we ever, Apple?"

"So how come we don't start?" she said.

Gag. The only thing more appetite-killing than Mom and

Dad fighting was Mom and Dad flirting. Apparently they'd made up. Inquiring minds did not need to know any more than that, thank you.

"You don't *have* to go to school today, you know, Morgan," Mom purred, running one hand up and down Dad's arm. "If you want to stay home and nap, or get your nails done . . ."

"Or play with power tools."

"What?" Mom and Dad both turned to me. Luckily they'd both been too busy acting like lovebirds to hear my wise-crack, though Tammy snorted milk out her nose in a most satisfactory way.

"I said, I'll go to school." I forced a smile. "That periodic chart of the elements is just starting to make sense to me. Don't want to miss it!"

"Mmm," said Mom and Dad at the same time. "Chemistry."

Gag.

School made the time pass, though a lot of the junior girls were absent and the ranks thinned even more as the day progressed. I spent the day obsessing about how I could present those magic shoes to Colin in a way that would actually make him put them on. That was the main thing on my mind, until I got home and opened the door to my closet.

Oh, *fek.*

My five dollar prom dress?

Gone.

In its place: pink pink pink. The Pepto-Bismol nightmare. The pink princess pukoid dress. And a note:

Oops! You forgot to pick up your dress! So we had it delivered. We wish you a delightful evening.

We are having the rest of your clothes cleaned and pressed in the meantime.

Some coordinated separates have been provided for your convenience! (Should you choose to keep any of them we will bill accordingly.)

Please tell your friends about our commitment to EXCELLENT service!

Your friends at,
Wee Folk Custom Tailors & Alterations

Coordinated separates? There were pink T-shirts. Pink sweaters. Pink yoga pants. Pink knit hats. Pink camisoles, pink oxford button-downs, pink skirts, pink jeans, pink hoodies and a really nauseating pink fake-fur coat.

And—the dress.

With only two and a half hours to get ready, I considered my options.

Option A) Race back to Strohman's and grab something, anything, off the rack, then show up at prom a sweaty, stressed-out wreck in a last-minute dress that might not even fit.

Option B) Embrace the irony, take a nap and a shower, put on the dress and some matching pink lipgloss and a "yes, I know how asinine I look" attitude and call it a choice.

For me, there was no choice, really. Option B was the only thing a semi-goddess *would* do.

I set my alarm, found a cozy pink nightgown in my dresser drawer, stretched out on the bed and fell asleep.

tammy, of course, loved my outfit—"it's perrrrrrrrfect! Just like a princess!" she squealed—and my parents were more or less speechless, but Mike's reaction when he came to pick me up practically made the whole dress-tastrophe worthwhile.

"Whoa," he said, taking it in. "*Whoa*. You look—Morgan, may I say something?" He got down on one knee, which cracked me up. "You are, without question, the most ironical girl ever in the history of girlness."

"Thank you." I curtsied with maximum irony. "That is an awesome compliment." My hair was still too short to do much more with than wash and fluff, but I'd added a dozen of Tammy's most sparkly barrettes and some hair product to spike it up in a few spots. Overall effect: Tinker-Bell punk. The see-through, high-heeled Cinderella sandals I'd found in my closet added a nice glass slipper effect. Naturally the shoes fit me perfectly.

And speaking of shoes, the box with Colin's new boots was too bulky to carry, so I'd put the boots in my school gym bag, an oversized duffel with the East Norwich High School emblem printed on the side.

"Got my purse," I said, swinging the gym bag over my bare shoulder. "Let's go do prom."

"Like it's never been done before." Mike grinned and held the door open for me.

"Oh! Hey, Mike," I said, before I forgot. "You look great too." And he did, naturally—what guy doesn't look great in a tux? But it was the hideous boots in my duffel bag that I most longed to see modeled on someone's feet.

the junior prom had a "no limo" rule to help keep the insanity in check, so Mike's dad dropped us off at the East Norwich Country Club. The other attendees were climbing out of cars too, a sea of familiar faces in a weirdly unfamiliar context. The guys looked a comical mix of proud and embarrassed in their formalwear, and the girls were squealing and hugging each other—gently, so as to not wreck the outfits— and exchanging compliments.

I got plenty of stares, but honestly, after the "what's up with the bald chick?" treatment I'd endured in September, nothing fazed me. My more urgent problem was figuring out how to transport my butt from the junior prom to the Spring Faery Ball. I was also keeping an eye out for Sarah, but Clementine and Deirdre saw me first, as Mike and I approached the entrance to the club.

"Oh my God," Clementine squeaked.

"Oh my *God*!" Deirdre shrieked. "You look—pink!"

"Yup," I said.

"Except for the corsage," Mike chimed in. The corsage was white, thankfully, which at least didn't clash.

"Nice—corsage," the girls both said at the same time.

Sarah, who was tall enough to see above the crowd and spot me from a distance, took one astonished look, screamed like she was on fire, and then sprinted over in her high heels and slapped me high fives, just like we were standing on the centerline of the basketball court.

"This is *subversive!*" she cheered, jumping up and down. "You are both stunning *and* hideous! You are embodying prom *and* mocking prom, all in the same moment! And the gym bag for a purse, it is *so* brilliant, Morgan. I love you forever and ever for this, and oh my God, *happy birthday!*" Sometimes Sarah went off the deep end with her theoretical musings, but that was part of her charm. Then she grabbed me by the shoulders. "But what happened to that killer dress we found at Strohman's?"

I wish I knew, I thought. "I'm saving it," I said, "for a special occasion."

As I entered the lobby, the compliments on my outfit were nonstop. Apparently, being Mike Fitch's date was giving me enough starter cool that this mind-bogglingly geeky getup was being seen as the last word in hip. Mike loved every minute of it, and beamed at everyone we passed.

"Awesome color."

"Love the barrettes."

"Oh my God, are those *really* glass slippers?"

The swirl of tuxedos and dresses was dizzying. I shifted the gym bag to my other shoulder and felt the weight of Colin's new boots. Every minute I stood there sopping up

my new princess-for-a-day status was another minute poor
Colin was stuck squiring real faery princesses around the
dance floor. *Enough of this,* I thought. *I need to find the entrance to my* real *prom.*

Please enter by the lobby fountain, the invitation to the
Faery Ball read. Finding the fountain was a cinch. Right in
the center of the lobby, lit by a thousand tiny halogen
pinspots, was the pride and joy of the East Norwich Country Club—the Kappock Fountain, donated by Kar-Krazy
Kappock himself, according to the brass plaque mounted on
the fountain's base.

Above, two life-sized, arching dolphins squirted water
high in the air. The area around the fountain was bathed in
cool mist, which meant all the newly fussed-over hairdos
were being kept at a safe distance.

I walked in a wide, slow circle around the fountain, looking for a crack, a seam, a knob, a trapdoor in the carpet—
anything that might be an entrance.

"Everything okay?" Mike asked. "You're, like, orbiting."

"Fine, fine," I said absently. "I was just wondering—you
know, where does the water come from? Where does it go?"

"It's called plumbing," Mike said, giving me a puzzled
look. "Pipes. Drains. Like in the bathroom."

"Drains, right," I said, smiling dumbly. "Duh. I think I
must have inhaled too much hairspray."

"If that's the case, why don't you stay here and detox
while I go pick up our seating assignment?"

On the other side of the lobby were tables staffed by par-
ent volunteers. They were giving out the place cards that told

everyone where to sit at dinner. At the moment, there were long lines at every table. *Perfect,* I thought. *That'll keep Mike out of my hair while I figure this out.*

"Thanks, Mike," I said. "You are an excellent prom date."

"This is just practice—wait until next year." He nodded at my heavy gym bag. "You want me to check that?"

"No!" It came out a little sharply, but I followed it up with a sweet, princessy smile. Mike shrugged and went off to stand in line.

Twice more I circumnavigated the fountain. *Come on, Morganne,* I urged my goddess half. *Open your eyes and see what's in front of you. It's got to be here somewhere.*

When I passed the Kar-Krazy Kappock plaque for the third time, that's when the dolphins piped up.

"Welcome!" one of them said, briefly interrupting the jet of water spraying from its blowhole. "May we direct you to the Spring Faery Ball?"

"Yes, please!" I said, barely hiding my surprise. "Where exactly is the entrance? I can't seem to find it."

"You're already here," the other dolphin explained. "Proceed straight through the fountain, yield at the yellow light, check all mirrors for oncoming traffic, then carefully merge into the Faery Ball."

"*Through* the fountain?" I exclaimed. "Are you kidding me? I just did my hair!"

They nodded their great smooth heads, just like the performing dolphins at SeaWorld do when the trainer waves a delicious fish treat in front of their noses. Then they honked and chirped and squeaked some encouragement, in their own strange and beautiful language.

Without daring to glance over my shoulder to see if any-one was watching, I clutched the gym bag holding Colin's magic boots to my pink-taffeta-wrapped chest, and stepped into the spray.

twenty-two

... a wet, pink rat...

... a pink cotton candy on a stick that got caught in the rain...

... a strawberry-iced cupcake that somebody spilled a carton of milk on...

Images of what my utterly destroyed outfit would look like when I stepped out of the fountain swirled in my mind, pink and disgusting, like an artificially flavored and colored raspberry milkshake going *down, down, down* the drain.

It doesn't matter, I thought, as the water hit me like a cold blast from a garden hose. *I am here to save Colin. Not to dazzle him with my ironic fashionista prom outfit.*

Inside the fountain, the dolphins were swimming corkscrews around me and smiling their wide, head-enveloping grins. The water was so full of bubbles and froth it was hard to see. It felt like we were spinning and sinking at the same time, but I wasn't sure which way was up anymore. Finally the dolphins stopped and chirped in unison.

"Jump!"

How was I supposed to jump, with nothing to push off of?

"Jump!" they repeated. "Like this!" With powerful swipes of their broad tails, they shot upward.

"Yield at the yellow light!" one of them called in a familiar, parental way, its squeaky voice fading as it soared and breached the surface. "Don't forget to check your mirrors!"

The water spun me around in the wake of the dolphins' sudden exit. Still holding the gym bag, I flutter-kicked my high-heeled feet as fast as I could, and followed.

Yield at the yellow light. . . .

Check all mirrors. . . .

Merge carefully into the Faery Ball. . . .

There was dry land beneath my feet. Dry marble, to be exact, in a luscious swirl of cream and yellow, like clouds passing over a lemon sky. The stone was worn smooth by centuries of dancing feet, and I noticed that the yellow markings formed a subtle dashed pattern, just like a merge lane onto the highway.

How gross it would be to drip a puddle of water onto this lovely floor, I thought. I hiked up the bottom of my dress and wondered if there was any chance of finding a towel somewhere, but the fabric of my dress was not dripping.

It wasn't even wet.

It wasn't even *pink*.

"Mor?" The voice I most wanted to hear rang out, echoing off the stone and straight into my heart. "Bloody hell, girl, is that really you? Or are these mischief-makers playing magical tricks upon me eyes?"

It was Colin, looking completely ridiculous in a powder blue tux, with a hugely ruffled shirt and tight bell-bottom trousers.

My Colin, staring at me in openmouthed surprise and pimped out in the top-of-the-line kitsch of seventies disco prom finery. It was the second most beautiful thing I'd ever seen in my life.

The first most beautiful thing, if you could believe the silver-framed, full-length mirror propped against the wall near where I was standing, was me. I was in the beige dress from Strohman's, except it was ten times as gorgeous as before and fully goddess-worthy—bedazzled with jewels, bedecked with flowers, trailing a gossamer train that floated as I walked. My hair, a yard long and shiny as polished copper, was piled like a princess's on top of my head, with the softest red-gold ringlets cascading around my ears.

And, okay. My boobs seemed a tad bigger than normal too.

Caution. My eyes followed my reflection down and saw the words inscribed in small letters at the bottom of the mirror. *Objects in mirror are foxier than they appear.*

The gym bag was still in my arms, and it was perfectly dry. I held it out to Colin.

"No time to explain," I said. "Would you put these on? Please?"

Looking confused, Colin unzipped the bag and gazed with horror upon its contents.

"Ugh! These've been beat with an ugly stick, for sure," he exclaimed. "I didn't think this outfit of mine could be made any more hideous, but clearly I was wrong."

"It would be totally excellent," I said, glancing around for any sign of an evil faery queen approaching, "if you could just put those boots on without us having a big conversation about it."

"Why's that?" he said. "And, pardon me language—but what the fek are we both doin' here in these fancy getups?" He looked me up and down. "I have to say, lass, I think you take the prize for best frock. My wardrobe's more in the ironic vein."

"Put on the boots," I begged, "and let's dance. Now."

He laughed bitterly. "No offense, Mor, but dancing's the last thing I'd do voluntarily at the moment."

"Finally!" A high, shrill voice snaked out like a lasso and caught us in midconversation. "The guest of honor is here!"

For the first time since emerging from the fountain, I looked around. Where Colin and I stood, the cool marble floor and stately stone walls shimmered under the flickering light of candelabra chandeliers (the kind with real candles, not those dumb flame-shaped light bulbs you see in East Norwich dining rooms). This medieval charm lasted for about fifty feet or so, then abruptly gave way to a dance floor that looked much more hard rock than medieval stone. A disco ball hung ironically above, like a mirrored, glittering moon, throwing rainbows of light across the dancers as it turned.

Walking toward us was Queen Titania, dressed in black leather pants, cuff bracelets and a band T-shirt that read "Faeries rock!" Her head was shaved on both sides and the center was glued up into a massive, liberty-spiked Mohawk. When she opened her mouth to speak, I saw a big silver stud pierced through the tip of her tongue.

"Happy birthday, darling!" She was lisping a little because of the stud. "I hope you like your party!"

"I—I thought this was the Spring Faery Ball." The fast, regular bass thump and shrieking guitar sound of heavy metal music started pounding from the dance floor.

"Oh, it's *that* too, I suppose." She waved a hand dismissively. "Same old ball every spring, pretty dresses and tiaras, ho, hum, yawn! This year I decided we should do something *different*! More *youthful*! In honor of your birthday! I just thought of it this morning." She twirled and showed off the back of her T-shirt, which read, "Who are *you* calling a faery?" in blood-soaked letters. "Do you like it? Do you think it's 'hip'?"

"It's, uh—hard core," I said, while thinking, *just get him in the shoes, that's all you need to do*. "Maybe Colin and I should go someplace and change into more appropriate outfits."

"No, you mustn't; you look adorable," she lisped. "We knew you'd be dressed for your silly human prom, and we wanted to make sure you and Colin matched, so we provided him with this *scrumptious* tuxedo. And, Colin, may I say— yum *yum*! That shade of pastel blue is *your* color." She patted her Mohawk delicately. "Now, come get a drink and have fun. The bartender is serving—I believe they're called Long Island Iced Teas." Her eyes flitted to the gym bag in Colin's arms. "But why don't we check your bag first? You don't want to lug *that* monstrosity around all night."

"It's mine. I'll hang on to it." I reached for it.

Before I could get the bag away from Colin, the queen grabbed it and looked inside.

"What exquisite boots," she cooed. "Are they yours?"

"Morgan just gave 'em to me," Colin said politely.

"How generous. I imagine you're eager to try them on, then." She glanced at me, and then at Colin. "But no no no, they don't match your tuxedo at all! You can try them on later. *After* the ball. I'm sure Morganne won't mind." She turned back to me, and her eyes shone like broken glass. "After all, there isn't anything *special* about those boots, is there, Morganne?"

Jolly Dan's warning played in my head—*if you tell him that they're magic, they won't work.* I gulped. "Nope," I said, "they're just boots."

"I'll put them away for now, then," she said, taking the bag away from Colin. "You should *never* break in new shoes at a dance, you know! It causes the most *excruciating* blisters."

Adorable or not, Colin and I didn't blend in very well with the other partygoers. I was stunning in my goddess outfit and he looked like an outtake from *Dumb and Dumber*, but all the other guests were dressed in various styles and eras of punk and heavy metal gear, just like Queen Titania.

Of course it couldn't be that simple, I thought to myself in frustration. *But just wait. There will be a way, some way, to get those boots on his feet.*

"Sorry I didn't say happy birthday!" Colin shouted over the music. "I've no sense at all what day it is. The music's brilliant, innit?"

It was, but the place was so packed I couldn't get a look at the band. It wasn't until they launched into a deafening rendition of "Rock and Roll All Nite" that Colin dragged me by the hand to a less-crowded spot at the edge of the dance floor, where we could actually see the stage.

"Bloody hell!" he cried. "That's Gene Simmons! The Bat Lizard himself!"

I looked, then blinked my eyes and looked again.

This was no tribute band. It was the genuine, ear-splitting, tongue-waggling thing.

Kiss was playing at my birthday ball.

I wasn't sure how I felt about that, but Colin was in heaven. "In the normal scheme of reality," he yelled in my ear, "those boys are a bunch of senior citizens now. To see them young, still together, in their prime . . . it's quite a treat, quite a treat." He sounded reverent. "Twenty-three consecutive gold records! Did ye know that? Only the Rolling Stones and the Beatles had more."

"That's great, Colin—hey!" Jolly Dan and Taffy were maneuvering hand-in-hand through the maze of dancing legs. Now they'd spotted me and were waving like mad. Jolly Dan was in black, except for a red-and-white striped Dr. Seuss hat that was as tall as he was, and Taffy had artfully distressed what looked like one of Tammy's old Cinderella costumes into a tattered, vampire-princess gown. Very Disneygoth.

The tiny couple found their way to us and I introduced them to Colin with care—after all, the first meeting between a skeptical Irishman and a pair of leprechauns was not a moment to be taken lightly.

"Son of a gun!" Colin sputtered. "First Gene Simmons and now this! Wait'll I tell me grandpap!"

"You both look awesome," I said to them. "Are you having fun?"

"The most fun I've ever had," Jolly Dan replied, his eyes crinkling with gratitude. "Did you check out the gnome sisters?"

He jerked his head and I looked in the direction his hat pointed to. Glenwyn and Drenwyn were standing on each other's shoulders, but even added together they still weren't nearly as tall as their arrogant elf-date.

"They've been taking turns being on top," Jolly Dan scoffed. "So far he doesn't seem to have noticed the difference."

"Who knew?" I shrugged. "I guess they're stackable."

"I tried to talk to them," Taffy said. "To tell them my, uh, news. They didn't care." She shook her head. "I always thought those two were kind of plastic."

Jolly Dan was staring at Colin's feet. "Surely," he said in a low voice, "a handsome gentleman like you could find some better-looking footwear than that?"

Colin looked down at the glitter-encrusted platform shoes that came with his tux. "Ye think these are bad?" he said, laughing. "Ye should've seen the ones that Mor—"

"Colin!" I shrieked, just to shut him up.

"What?"

"I. Um. I. Um." My making-up-lame-excuses powers seemed to have deserted me, so I settled for a distraction instead and pointed at the stage. "Look!"

Queen Titania was grabbing the microphone from Gene Simmons, right in the middle of a song. "Birthday cake!" she

screamed into the mike. The drummer punctuated her an-
nouncement with an explosive riff. Rivers of smoke poured
onto the dance floor, and there was a burst of flame.

Everyone screamed, but the fire turned out to be poor
Finnbar, tottering under the weight of a huge birthday cake
that was covered with hundreds of blazing candles.

"Whew," he panted, putting the cake down on the edge
of the stage. "This is getting hot!"

Queen Titania saw the questioning look on my face. "In
faery years," she explained, "you're quite a bit older than seventeen. In fact, you're vastly older than young Colin here."
She frowned at the cake. "Next year we'll do one candle per
century, I think. It's starting to get very cluttered, and I can't
abide clutter!"

Clutter? I looked at the queen, and in a sickening flash I
realized what felt so familiar about her. It wasn't just that she
was the spitting image of Mrs. Blainsvoort. There was something else—something that should have been obvious—

"Oh fek!" I choked out. "Are you my faery goddess-
mother?"

She smiled. "Silly Morganne! I knew you'd remember
eventually!"

"See?" Finnbar grinned. "We really are brother and sister!
Now blow out your candles and make a wish."

A wish? Figuring out my family tree would have to wait.
"If I make a wish, will it definitely come true?" I asked the
queen.

"My dear daughter," she said, not seeming the least bit
worried, "a half-goddess's birthday wish *always* comes true."

Then I wish for Colin to not dance at the faery balls anymore,
I almost blurted, but I caught myself.

It's too easy. Magical faery-mommy or not, Queen Titania
was not what I would consider a nice person. She could make
my no-more-dancing wish come true by turning Colin into
something without legs, like an earthworm or a slug.

I wish—

I wish for—

I thought so hard my head hurt. *It's a trick,* I realized in
despair. Any wish I came up with would be far too easy for
the queen to twist into something awful.

I looked around at the sea of punk and goth and heavy
metal faeries staring at me impatiently. Colin watched me
too. His cornflower-blue eyes were nearly the same color as
his tux. I had to admit, he seemed quite at home among the
faery folk by now. Had things gone too far for me to put
them right?

Even Gene Simmons was looking at me. The black-and-
white demon paint on his face was harmlessly clownlike, now
that he was just another musician on a gig, milling about between sets as if playing a faery ball was all in a day's work.
Though maybe it was, to him.

That's what gave me the answer.

Follow the KISS rule, I thought, remembering one of my
dad's more annoying sayings. *Keep it simple, stupid. Remember
what Jolly Dan told you to do. Stick to the plan.*

"I wish," I said carefully, "for Colin to put on the new
boots I gave him earlier this evening."

And, with an enormous, half-goddess breath that I didn't

know I had in me, I blew out every one of those hundreds of candles.

There was a smattering of lukewarm applause at my boring wish. Quick as a flash, Finnbar raced to the coat check to get the gym bag.

"I had to tip her a couple of bucks," he whispered to me, as he laid the bag at Colin's feet. "You can pay me back later, 'kay, sis?"

With everyone watching, Colin unzipped the bag and took out the boots. A collective *ooooooh* of admiration rose from the crowd. I caught Jolly Dan's eye; he was on the dance floor, trapped in a sea of legs and looking ten feet tall with pride.

Colin kicked off the glittering platform shoes and put on the boots.

One spin, I saw Jolly Dan mouth at me, from knee-level. I hurled myself at Colin and spun him right around so fast he didn't know what hit him.

"Do they fit?" asked the queen, falsely sweet as a pound of aspartame.

"They fit—perfectly," Colin said, like a person waking from a dream. "I'd say they're the best fittin' shoes I've ever worn, if I was forced to pick." He looked around slowly, seeing it all for the first time. Then he spotted me.

"Morgan! What are ye doing in Dublin? And what club is this? I don't recognize it." He rubbed his eyes. "To be honest, I don't remember goin' clubbin' to begin with. I was just home in me own bed, readin' *Popular Robotics.*"

"The shoes fit perfectly," the queen repeated, sounding deeply disappointed. "How very Cinderella. Ah, well. We'll miss you, Colin. But at least you were here for Morganne's birthday. That's all that matters, I suppose."

"And there'll be no further mischief, with this boy or any other," Jolly Dan bellowed to no one in particular. "Not unless all of ye want to dance barefoot for the rest of your immortal faery lives."

All the partygoers hung their heads, and Queen Titania glared at me as if she might reduce her own daughter to ash with a single crook of her finger. Even the disco ball stopped turning. Then, sudden as a lightning strike, she threw both hands in the air and whooped.

"Mosh pit!" she yelled. The band was already in position, and Gene Simmons counted off into a screaming metal version of "Some Day My Prince Will Come," from the *Snow White* movie. The disco ball swept a rainbow searchlight around the room, and the party came back to life as if nothing had happened—except now, of course, everyone was eating birthday cake.

Colin stared at me as if he would never look away, and I saw the wonder in his eyes. "Damn, Morgan," he said. "You look fantastic."

"Thanks." I grinned. "So do you."

He rocked on his heels for a moment, shoved his hands into the pockets of his powder-blue polyester pants, and smiled shyly. "You wanna dance?"

"I'd love to," I said. "And then we're going home."

"the crowd at this club, it's a bit mallcore, if you ask me," Colin shouted, as we struggled to stay together on the dance floor. "Though I can't complain, not with Gene Simmons thrashin' away for our personal entertainment! Before becoming a mainstay of reality television the man was a true musical legend, y'know. It's like seein' bloody Sinatra at the Sands."

It was a great party, I had to admit. Now Jolly Dan and Taffy were stage diving like rock stars, and the crowd was loving it.

"Colin," I yelled over the din. "Can we slow dance?"

"What?"

I cupped my mouth with my hands and yelled louder. "Slow dance! Can we?"

"The music is hardly suitable," he shouted back.

"I don't care." I put my arms around his neck, in classic slow dance position. "It's just that I had this wish that you'd be able to take me to my junior prom, and I know you can't, and anyway, it's tonight, and you'll wake up in Ireland in a few minutes and won't remember any of this, but . . ." I looked up and gazed pleadingly into his eyes. "Just—humor me, okay?"

"I can manage that," Colin said, right next to my ear. "A slow dance it is."

So, with Gene Simmons and Kiss rocking their highly amplified guts out, and an assortment of pierced and tattooed magical beings pogoing and body-slamming all around us, Colin and I slow danced. As soon as I felt his arms around me, we could have been anywhere—a moonlit beach, the top of Mount Everest or the middle of Grand Central Station at rush hour—and I wouldn't have noticed. Or cared.

"Seventeen, eh? Yer still too young for me, ye know," he said, after a while.

"Ha," I retorted. "That excuse is bogus. I'm much older than you in faery years."

"Happy birthday, then, you older woman, you." He held me tighter. "I wish I had a present for ye."

"You do," I said impulsively. I stood on tiptoe and whispered something in his ear.

"Are you sure that's wise?"

"Why?"

"Because, according to you, I won't remember it. How's that gonna feel, eh? When I act like it never happened? Ye know I'm not that kind of bloke."

"I'll remember it, though," I said. "For both of us."

Taking a step back from me, he started patting the pockets of his tux. "I'll write meself a note, then." He found a pen and, on the back of his left hand, he drew a big heart and wrote inside it:

On the occasion of her
17th birthday
Colin
kissed
Morgan

He tucked the pen back into his pocket. Then he kissed me. It was, whoa. I mean, *whoa*.

As we kissed, I slid my arms around his neck again, and somehow the music magically turned into "Can You Feel the

Love Tonight" from *The Lion King*, which would have been awesomely promlike except it sounded like the William Hung version, but we didn't care because we weren't dancing anymore.

It turns out a kiss in the faery realm can last as long as you want. A moment, a night, a year—even a whole magical lifetime.

It was all the birthday present I wanted.

twenty-three

Word spread around the junior prom quicker than cribbed answers to the chemistry final—*Morgan jumped in the fountain! Morgan jumped in the fountain!*

Do I even have to say what happened next? Sarah and Dylan led the way, right before appetizers were served. Clem and Deirdre (together, of course) took their turn when the entrees came. Then people started to get it. Before the evening was through, nearly every student at prom, singly or in couples or in groups of three or four, "accidentally" fell into the Kappock Fountain. So simple, so harmless and yet, in terms of completely freaking out the chaperones, and especially Mrs. Blainsvoort, so very, very effective.

At least, that's what Sarah told me the next day. I wasn't there to witness the soggy triumph of the East Norwich High School junior class over the forces of boringness. All I knew was that by the time Mike had returned with our seating assignments, I was sprawled on my butt in the water, wearing a sopping pile of pink taffeta and a look of sheer bliss on my face.

"Morgan!" He sprinted toward me, letting the place cards flutter to the ground. "What happened? Are you okay?"

My dress was soaked, my hair was plastered to my head, my mascara was running in rivulets down my cheeks and dripping brown-black Maybelline spots on the bodice of my dress. "I was tossing a penny in the fountain," I sputtered, as the water streamed down my face. "I guess I lost my balance."

"Well," he said, after a moment, "I hope you made a wish."

This started me laughing so hard I couldn't stand up. And Mike, who was trying to drag slippery me out of the water, started laughing too, and before you could say, *Keep It Subversive, Stupid*, he tumbled into the fountain after me.

We sat there, the two of us, laughing hysterically, with two enormous dolphins happily pouring water on our heads.

"Mike," I said, when I could catch my breath. "What do you say we blow this party off, go back to my house and watch TV?"

To Mike's credit, he didn't look one bit offended. Quite the opposite, in fact.

"Add pizza and I'm in," he said, wiping the water out of his eyes.

So that's what we did. My parents came to pick us up and, admirably, didn't ask an excessive number of questions. We hung our wet prom finery on the shower curtain rod to dry (it was kind of funny seeing Mike in my dad's sweatpants and old First Bank of Connecticut T-shirt) and ordered a pepper-

oni pie with extra cheese. We even let Tammy rule the remote
for a while, which got us stuck watching a Discovery Channel
show about dolphins. Luckily the pizza came soon after, and
we were spared any further Deep Thoughts about the "flip-
pered wonders of the sea."

Afterward, Mike said he'd like to meet up with the gang
for the planned after-prom breakfast, but I passed on it.

"Are you sure?" he said. "We can stick a birthday candle in
your pancakes."

I thought of Colin, and how he was probably soundly and
deeply asleep that very minute, with no dreams to trouble
him but the normal, everyday kind of dreams people have.
Who knows? Maybe he was even dreaming of me.

"Truthfully, Mike," I said, "it's been a long day, and I'd really rather go to bed."

i caught the fiercest cold the night of prom. it started
on Friday as a scratchy throat, but over the weekend it blos-
somed into a sniffling, feverish festival of misery. By Monday, the new Subversive Goddess of the junior class was
much too sick to go to school.

Dad had a job interview (second one for the same job, so
things were looking up), and Tammy was off to another day
of exchanging misinformation with Marcus in Miss Wallace's
class, but Mom offered to cancel her client meetings and stay
home. I said no. I'd be fine. I was going to snooze and blow
my nose and read fashion magazines and think.

I had a lot to think about, frankly.

Queen Titania? My faery goddess-mother?

I'd been told the story when I was in Ireland, of how the half-goddess Morganne was the child of a mortal man and a faery mother. The mortal man had been dead for eons by now, of course. I guess it never occurred to me that Magic Mom might still be around.

Boy, this is definitely a different spin on the "Heather has two mommies" concept, I thought. What was I supposed to do now? Send Queen Titania a mother's day card through the faery mail once a year? She was definitely the kind of person you had to watch your back around. Poor Finnbar seemed terrified of her.

It made me worry about him, which was ridiculous since he was just as capable of causing magical mischief as she was. Still, he was my little half-brother in the faery realm—I knew that for certain now—and family is family.

After I got tired of thinking and bored with the magazines—there were some nice clothes and all, but I'd had my fill of dresses for the moment—I surfed the 'Net. Then I sent Colin an e-mail, nothing major, just *I'm home sick and what's up with you*, that kind of thing.

I missed him, I really did, but not in that crazed, does-he-love-me-or-doesn't-he kind of way. Thanks to the weirdest birthday party ever, now I knew exactly how Colin felt about me. He might not remember all of it, yet, but he would. Someday he would.

Colin wrote back about an hour later. Big surprise: He was feeling miraculously, one-hundred percent better and sleeping like a baby. The annoying campaign of "pocket adverts" seemed to be over as well.

This part made me crack up:

Bad luck about your sniffles. Perhaps it's good we re-
strained ourselves from getting too affectionate during
my visit, I'd feel awful if I thought I'd given you whatever nasty bug I had.

Then he went on:

My lackluster performance in the robotics competition
failed to impress the DCU scholarship committee
(shocking news). So, unless something better comes
along, I'll be working the bike tour again this summer,
to make tuition for next year. It'd be good fun if you
came, but you may well have better things to do, and if
so I totally understand.

Feel better, luv—
Colin

p.s.—how was the dance? & where's my photo?

Bloody hell, I thought. How could I send Colin the photo
I'd promised? Nobody had thought to snap a picture of me
on my ass in the fountain, and even if they had I didn't think
that was the kind of shot he had in mind.

My real clothes had reappeared in my closet and drawers
on prom night, while I slept, all cleaned and pressed—
including the Strohman's dress. Would it be worth it to get all
prommed up again and have Sarah take a picture of me to
send to Colin? Or would that be too much like lying?

I was mulling this over when the doorbell rang. Even

though I was seventeen now, years of being warned never to answer the door when I was home alone had taken their toll. First I threw a sweater on over my pajamas, and then I peeked out the front window to see who it was. Across the green, uncluttered expanse of our lawn, I saw the FedEx truck pulling away.

I figured it was probably something for my mom, from one of her clients. Then I stepped outside to pick up the package and saw what the truck had delivered.

Eight good-sized crates (each one big enough to hold, say, two pairs of garden gnomes) were neatly stacked next to the garage. The crates had air holes and were stamped PERISHABLE, and the return name and address on the FedEx label was T. Smoothcheck, c/o Ace Ministorage.

Maybe I should open the boxes, I thought. But then I decided against it. This was a situation Mom and Dad would have to sort out for themselves.

It wasn't until I headed back inside the house that I noticed the flat FedEx envelope propped next to the front door. This one was addressed to me, with no return address. *It's probably something tedious from the College Board,* I tried to convince myself, as I removed a stiff white envelope from inside the FedEx packaging, *or the Connecticut Department of Motor Vehicles.*

It wasn't. The envelope read:

Your photos are ready.

I tore open the flap. There were two photos inside. Gently I slid the first one out and removed it from its glassine cover.

It was a prom photo of Colin and me. Me in my goddess gown, with my long princess hair piled on my head, him in his powder blue tux and magically ugly buckled boots. We were holding hands and we both looked completely, perfectly happy.

Should I send it to him? I wondered. He did ask for my prom picture, though I was sure it never occurred to him that he'd be in it. And, to be honest, I looked like a zillion bucks in that dress, and I kind of wanted him to see it.

Correction: I was dying for him to see it. But if I sent him the photo, there'd be an awful lot of explaining to do, and most of it would be stuff that Colin would find very, very hard to believe.

It's when ye like people, Colin had said to me once, in Ireland, *that ye should be most willin' to tell 'em the truth about yerself.*

Fine, whatever. I can decide later, I thought, as I put that picture aside and took the second photo out of the envelope.

This one I had to stare at for a minute.

The second photo was—

Okay. Even I found this hard to believe.

The location was unmistakable. The photo was of my living room, in my house. There was my Christmas tree, with all the goofy ornaments Tammy and I had made over the years.

And there was Santa Claus: red suit, white beard, round belly, grinning and winking at the camera and sliding something under the tree.

In the background, but clearly visible in the photo: me, stretched out on the sofa, eyes closed, *The Magical Tales of Ireland* propped on my chest.

Oh fek, I thought. *Wait until Tammy sees this.*

about the author

Maryrose Wood has yet to find the perfect dress, but it's so fun to keep looking. There are also shoes to be considered.

Maryrose wrote *Why I Let My Hair Grow Out*, *Sex Kittens and Horn Dawgs Fall in Love* and *My Life: The Musical*. Visit her at www.maryrosewood.com.